UNTIL SERENA

A SMALL TOWN ROMANCE

CHIQUITA DENNIE

304 PUBLISHING COMPANY

Until Serena

For questions and comments about this book, please contact 304 Publishing Company at info@chiquitadennie.com Visit the official website at www.chiquitadennie.com

 Formatted with Vellum

INTRODUCTION

Grab some wine and get ready for more spicy, sinful, sexy romance!

Have you signed up for my newsletter?

Join today and find out all the latest new releases, contests, giveaways, sneak peeks, and more!

www.chiquitadennie.com

LATEST RELEASES FROM CHIQUITA DENNIE

Series

Struck in Love

The Early Years-A Prequel Short Story

Ruthless: Antonio and Sabrina Book 1

Savage: Antonio and Sabrina Book 2

Beastl: Antonio and Sabrina Book 3

Captivated By His Love: Janice and Carlo

Brutal: Antonio and Sabrina Booke 4

Redemption: Antonio and Sabrina Book 5

Heart of Stone

Broken, Book 1 (Emery & Jackson)

A Valentine's Day Short Book 1.5 Emery & Jackson

Rebirth, Book 2 (Jordan and Damon)

Reveal, Book 3 (Angela and Brent)

Bottoms Up Book 3.5 Jessica and Joseph Short

Renew, Book 4 (Jessica and Joseph)

Cocky Billionaire Boys

Cocky Catcher (Cocky Billionaire Boys Book 1)

Bossy Billionaire (Cocky Billionaire Boys Book 2)

The Fuertes Cartel

Stolen (The Fuertes Cartel Book 1)
Saved (The Fuertes Cartel Book 2)
Betrayed (The Fuertes Cartel Book 3)

Carrington Cartel

Torn: The Carrington Cartel Book 1
Claim: The Carrington Cartel Book 2

Something

Something Gained: A Romantic Comedy Book 1
Something Earned: A Romantic Comedy Book 2

Pierce Motors

Refuel:(Pierce Motors Book l)
Pressure:(Pierce Motors Book 2)
Ride: (Pierce Motors Book 3)

Summer Break

Summer Nights (Summer Break Book 1)

TN Seal Security

Aydin: Book 1
Nasir: Book 2
Nicco: Book 3

Standalones

Until Serena
Temptation
She's All I Need
I Deserve His Love

AUTHOR INSPIRATION

Author Inspiration

"Never dim your light to let someone else shine."

—Chiquita Dennie

DISCLAIMER

This work of fiction contains strong language and explicit sexual content and is only intended for mature readers. This story may contain unconventional situations, language, and sexual encounters that may offend some readers. If you're looking for sweet, fluffy romance, I would recommend another book. This book is for mature readers (18+).

PLAYLIST

SYNOPSIS

Serena is determined to build a good life for herself and her twin boys following a devastating breakup. Fiercely independent and prideful, she's doing everything she can to keep them afloat and not ask for help. That plan works out fine until Mother Nature, crying kids, a car that breaks down, and a sexy Alpha male with enough cockiness to make her swoon, collide and force her to leave her comfort zone.

Khalil has two focuses: his career at the investment firm and enjoying single life. That would be a lot easier if his meddling parents would stop trying to fix him up with high-society locals. He just might get his wish when he stumbles upon an accident and meets the woman who can make him change his outlook and possibly get him to settle down.

Find out what happens when a feisty woman meets her match in the anti-prince charming! Will it lead to a happily ever after?

1

———

SERENA

Once I finished my shift at Savory, I decided it would be easier to pick up groceries, then come straight to the boy's school to cut my time in half to pick them up, rather than go home to change clothes and deal with the kids fighting in the store. Silas and Prince were completely opposite in personality, but they both could cause an uproar if I didn't give in to them. It was partially my fault because my ex Jaylen, their father, wasn't consistent in their lives when we were together. Once I finally got the courage to leave, he was even less involved with co-parenting because he wanted to punish them, to force me to come back to him.

The weather started out with a cool breeze and light sun, as I drove away from the school to head home. I hit the turn signal from the main road to go onto the highway and head back quicker while the boys fought over the bag of grapes when drizzle started to pour down. I hated driving in this weather because people didn't understand how to be cautious versus driving like maniacs. I turned the music down low and glanced in the rearview mirror as Prince stole a grape out of Silas' hand. I shook my head at them as a splash of water hit the driver's side of the car, and Silas cried.

"Mommy! Mommy!" Silas yelled, trying to claw at his brother.

"Prince, be nice to your brother," I replied and moved onto the off-ramp toward the connecting freeway to our home. All of a sudden, I heard a loud grumbling noise from my car, and smoke seeped out. It didn't help that this car, bought six months ago from a used lot, was all I could afford at the time since moving to NorthPark, Tennessee for a fresh start. Jaylen was still in Nashville with the woman he left me for and started a new family with, based on the messages I'd seen pop up on my phone.

"He started it," Prince whined. My twins were in the first grade, so everything was always heightened with them.

"Please don't start! Damn it," I mumbled under my breath, dropping my head back on the seat.

"Ooh, Mommy said a bad word," Prince said, giggling to his brother.

Out the corner of my eye, Silas grabbed the bag of grapes out of his hand.

"Sorry, baby," I groaned, rubbing the back of my neck. It was really coming down, and I still had another fifteen minutes before we made it home. I tried to think positive and prayed the car would keep going before it completely died on me. It was a 2005 four-door Corolla. I had to borrow the money from my parents and best friend Dionne who worked at the school the boys attended. My parents weren't Jaylen's biggest fans. After a short time, I was able to move out of their place. I was tired of taking handouts and having to be under their rules while they tried to dictate my life. I was twenty-eight years old and starting over again as a single mom. Even with stress from bills piling up, on top of trying to spend time with my kids, I wouldn't change my decision to move on.

Pop!

And... that was the sound of my day getting even worse as the tire blew out on me, and the boys screamed at each other. The car swirled back and forth as I tried to get a handle on it to maneuver on the shoulder to safety.

"Give me the grapes, Silas!" Prince shouted.

"No!" Silas screamed.

I finally pulled my car over to the side of the road, close to an embankment, as the cars drove on. I was exhausted, hungry, and needed a long bath and a glass of wine to get this day over. I turned to look over my shoulder and see what all the fighting was about.

"Can't you two share without fighting?" I asked them with a pleading eye.

Both of them had dried tears and gave me puppy dog eyes.

"Sorry, Mommy." Silas bit another one.

I reached back to take the leftover bag of grapes and split them up between the two. When I jumped in surprise from a knock on the window I placed the grapes down in the passenger seat and wiped my hands on my skirt. I peered in my rearview mirror and saw a red Maserati behind me. A second knock came on my window.

"Lady, I'm trying to help you," he explained as he motioned for me to turn the window down. The heavy beating of the raindrops, cars honking, people yelling, and the kids crying in the back overwhelmed me. I was ready to explode at the same time. I was scared to be stuck out here with my kids waiting on AAA or someone to come. I grabbed my phone from my purse, prepared to dial my friend Dionne's number.

"I was about to call for help." I lifted my phone to see it was dead. I glanced back at the window toward the deep, raspy voice and rolled the window down. The rain continued to pour down, soaking him and getting into the car.

He pointed at my phone. "Looks like your phone is dead," he responded, cupping his jacket tighter.

"Uhm... I already called them before it died," I lied and dropped the phone to the side.

"Mommy, I'm hungry," Silas whimpered.

I whipped around to check on him. "Baby, we'll be home soon," I mentioned and looked through the bag in the seat for any extra snacks.

"I was behind you and saw your car swerving, then the tire went out," he spoke as he bent down and glanced to the backseat at my boys.

I wiped a hand across my face and sighed. "Yeah, the tire went out." I floundered at the brilliance of his look.

He stared back at me. "I can take you to my friend's shop to get your tire fixed." He wiped a hand down his legs, standing back up.

"You don't have to do that. I have someone coming." Nervously, my mind was congested with doubts and fears. The only man that I could depend on was my father and even when he complained about me needing to upgrade my car and offered to buy me one and I shut it down, I knew he was reliable. If I took him up on his offer, would he really not want anything in return?

"Mommy, I'm hungry," Prince complained.

"Okay, baby. Just give me a second," I said, looking up

the road and behind me, biting my bottom lip and trying to think of an alternative.

"Are you coming with me or are you going to try to be superwoman and stick it out?" he questioned, rubbing his hands together.

"I didn't ask you for help," I muttered snarkily, giving him a hostile glare.

He waved to my boys. "You two are hungry?" he asked my boys in the backseat.

"Yes!" Silas and Prince said at the same time.

I narrowed my eyes. "Boys, didn't I tell you to never talk to strangers?" I stated.

"He's no stranger." Silas grinned, trying to hand his grapes to the stranger.

I nudged him back in his seat. "Baby, be quiet and let me think."

"Listen, I can drive you to the shop, and you can call your friend from there." His tone was chided, holding up both hands showing he came in peace.

I nodded, giving up on any other idea to get out of this mess. I pushed my phone and the leftover snacks in my purse and unlocked my door. I stepped out, shut the door, and came face to face with the most handsome man I'd ever seen. I felt butterflies in my stomach and a lump in my throat. He stood around six foot three compared to my five-seven stature. I cleared my throat, slowly he backed up to give me room and I went toward the backseat to open the door and helped Prince and Silas out of their seats. They both jumped down and grabbed their jackets.

I helped Silas put his jacket on. "Stop jumping around, Silas." I ran a hand over his short curls. "I'm Serena. These are my boys Silas and Prince." I gripped both their hands.

He slipped a hand out for me to take. "Khalil. Do you need me to grab their car seats?" he asked. I mumbled yes and headed toward the trunk to grab the two bags of groceries, while he went for the back passenger seat to get my kids' car seats.

I guided the boys to stay off from the main road. "Wait right here, boys." I picked up the bags and my backpack with the receipts inside for my baking business. I slammed it shut and watched as he transferred the seats to his car. The boys followed and jumped inside, helping them to buckle up.

I dropped my purse on the floor and scrubbed a hand down my leg, looking back to check on my babies. "Thanks for helping. I'll pay you for gas," I offered, with a smile, ready to get home.

"Don't worry about it," he answered as he turned the heater on, then grabbed my bags and put them in his trunk.

"I can't do that. I owe enough people." I swallowed hard, a shadow of alarm touched my face.

His brow lifted in annoyance. "Did I ask for money?" he questioned and pulled his seatbelt on.

I followed, placing mine on. I was able to finally study him, from his large hands to his heart shaped lips to his low-cut fade. "No, but like I said, I don't want to owe you."

His gaze lowered, as did his voice, ignoring my statement.

"Mommy, are we home yet?" Prince asked.

"Not yet, baby. Soon," I answered.

Not soon after, we pulled into an auto shop. Khalil jumped out of the car and walked inside. As soon as I opened the door, the rain stopped, and the sun shined just as he walked back out with a familiar face.

"I forgot your name, but this is Arvon, a friend of mine," he said, slipping a hand in his pocket.

The little glimpse in the car did him no justice, from deep dark mahogany brown skin, in the dark grey, double-breasted suit. His bushy brows squinted at me, as he licked his lips and snapped his finger in front of my face.

I blushed in embarrassment. "Hi, Arvon. I didn't know you two knew each other." I leaned over and gave him a hug. The boys in the back yelled out Arvon's name. I met him through my friends Dionne and Nori.

Arvon chuckled, crossing his arms. "Yeah, we met through Wasim when Khalil needed someone to look at the car dealership he was thinking of purchasing," Arvon spoke.

"You work at Savory?" Khalil inquired.

I looked down at my uniform and nodded, not wanting to go into my life story.

"Khalil said your car broke down on the freeway." Arvon wiped the dirt off his hands with a rag. He was just as tall as Khalil.

"Mommy! Mommy!" Prince and Silas shouted.

I turned to face my boys. "I need to get home and get them fed. Arvon, do you mind if I use your phone to call a cab?" I started to reach for any cash in my pocket to pay him.

Khalil removed his keys. "I can drop you off." Khalil walked back to the car.

Arvon wrapped a hand around my shoulder. "I trust Khalil. He's a good guy. How many times did we say you needed a new car?" His smile disarmed me.

Khalil offering to help again made me feel guilty from pulling him away from whatever he had to do today. He was driving a Maserati for god's sake, he was way out of my league and probably felt sorry for me.

I waved him off. "Don't start with me, Arvon." He was like a big brother to me since we met a few months back.

"She's stubborn, I see. Arvon, she's parked ten minutes away at the off-ramp." Khalil stepped to the passenger side, held it open and waited.

I wanted to throw a tantrum like my kids but ignored the heated stare from Khalil.

"I've been there before. Let me get it towed before the rain starts up again," Arvon said as he went back into the garage.

I walked over and got in the car, beyond annoyed to be dealing with hungry kids screaming in the backseat, a broken-down car, and a stranger who thought he knew me enough to call me stubborn. I put my seatbelt back on, rolled my eyes, slumped back in the seat and he walked around to get in the other side. Once he locked the door, I could feel his eyes darted in my direction before reversing out of the parking lot as I looked out the window, biting my nail. It was a bad habit that I'd had since I was a kid trying to keep my attitude in check. On top of being this close, his cologne still filled the air even with the hard rain that had him outside my window earlier.

"Hey, hey, put your address in here," Khalil said, snapping his fingers in front of my face.

I blinked, then focused my gaze. "What?"

He motioned toward the navigation system, and I typed my address in.

"I know that area; you live near Nori and Harmony," Khalil said.

"It was the most reasonably priced place I could afford when I moved here seven months ago." I shrugged, laying my hands in my lap.

Khalil turned his head from the road to look at me. "So,

you're not originally from North Park?" Khalil questioned as he turned off from the left lane and headed down the street toward my building.

I bit my bottom lip, wondering how much detail to give. I figured we wouldn't see each other after the car ride, but at the same time we know some of the same people in town. "My parents and ex live in Nashville. I came out here for a new start."

"Mommy, can we have burgers tonight?" Prince asked.

I pointed in front of the grey brick building. "Right here is fine," I informed him, peering in the back to check on my boys, sighing ready to be in bed. Feeling the day consume me, I thought of what I could do about my car.

Khalil parked in front and turned his car off, watching me.

I opened the door and removed my seatbelt, focusing on my boys and avoiding eye contact with the sexy stranger. "Prince, wait until we get inside, baby."

"Lil dude is hungry," Khalil commented, pushing his door open.

I waved him off. "You don't need to help, I got it," I said as I pulled the back door wide. I helped Prince, then Silas out of the car, grabbed their seats, and put them on the ground. The boys ran toward the door, laughing and playing.

"Stop fussing, woman, and let me help you," Khalil replied, popping the trunk to grab our bags.

"The food is probably spoiled by now," I mumbled and picked up the car seats before I headed toward the door. I grabbed keys out of my purse to unlock the door, so the boys could run inside. "Slow down, you two," I fussed, shaking my head at their energy being on ten.

Khalil stepped up behind me. "Where do you want these?" Khalil probed.

"You can drop them on the table over there. Thank you." I pointed to the coffee table in front of the couch. I needed him to hurry up and leave because his presence was doing something to me I could not explain.

I put the car seats near the door, removed my jacket, and kicked off my shoes.

"All right, you're all set. You need anything else?" Khalil challenged.

"No, you've helped enough," I said as the boys ran up to me and wrapped their arms around my left and right leg.

Khalil pulled out a business card from inside his breast pocket and handed it to me. I took it, reading off the title. "Harrison Investment and Associates."

I looked up at him, flipping the card back and forth. "What do I need this for?"

"If you need a ride in the morning, my number's on the back," Khalil mentioned, extending his hand to open the door.

"Bye, Khalil!" Prince and Silas said at the same time.

I kissed my teeth. "I can call a cab. I don't take handouts," I said to him as he walked out of my apartment.

Khalil paused, leaning his head to the side. "I don't do handouts, and I'm not trying to step on your toes," Khalil said, standing next to his car before getting inside, while I stood in the doorway with my arms crossed over my chest.

"Thanks for the offer, but we'll be fine," I stated and went to close the door as he pulled into traffic. I closed the door with my back to it and caught my long-held breath.

I stared at the business card. "He was cute," I whispered to myself as I ran a hand down my face.

The boys filled the room with laughter. "Mommy, I'm cute," Silas said, running around the couch behind Prince.

"Yes, you are, baby." I moved off the door, picked up the groceries, and walked into the kitchen. I had a three-bedroom, two-bath apartment with a large kitchen and dining room connected. As soon as Dionne found this place and sent me the pictures, I put a security deposit to hold it until I could travel down. It was modestly decorated with some of the furniture from the old place I had with Jaylen. I took out the cheese, ground beef, and bread to prepare burgers and fries for dinner. Normally, I wouldn't have this on a school night, but I was still drained from the long day. I heard the TV turn on and felt a little bit of relief. They'd be preoccupied to give me enough time to start the food and change clothes. After washing my hands, I picked up the saucepan and turned on the stove as I placed the rest of the groceries away, tossing the bags in the trash. Then trekked over to make sure the boys were good, kissed them both on top of their head and went into my bedroom five minutes later to change when my house phone rang. I answered as I unbuttoned my uniform.

I smiled seeing my best friend calling. "Hey." I placed it against my ear.

"I've been calling you all afternoon," Dionne argued.

I pulled open my dresser and picked up a grey long sleeve shirt and sleeper pants. I changed in the bathroom and removed my brows. "My phone died on my way to pick up the boys." I slid my feet inside my pants, put on my house shoes, then turned to leave the bedroom to finish cooking.

I paused talking. "Boys, go wash up. Dinner will be ready soon."

"Okay, Mommy," Silas and Prince said at the same time as they jumped up to wash their hands.

"I can hear you're stressed," Dionne said.

"My car broke down, the boys were fighting, and then the rain poured down hard." A wry smile was hidden from all the bullshit I knew I would have to handle if my car cost too much to fix.

"How did you get back home?" Dionne inquired.

I placed the phone on speaker. "This guy helped us," I answered, turning the stove low.

"What guy? Was he cute? Did he seem cool?" Dionne ran off question after question.

I tossed the patties on the stove and put the fries in the air fryer as the boys came into the kitchen. I removed the plates from the cabinet, then picked up three glasses to set the table. "His name is Khalil and no, we didn't talk that long for me to get a full evaluation on him," I informed. Dionne would be ready to marry me off in a split second if she knew how Khalil looked.

"He dropped you off at home and if you took your normal route, that's about a ten-minute drive," Dionne insisted.

I froze at her statement. "And?"

"Enough time to get to know somebody. Khalil? Khalil Harrison?" Dionne repeated.

I put the phone on mute, grabbed the bread, and cut some tomatoes, onions, and lettuce, then unmuted. "You know him?" I headed to the fridge, grabbed the leftover pitcher of sweet tea, and poured them both a glass. A stab of a feeling, pulse pounding uncertainty, filled my chest if they were close.

"He's the son of stuck-up Samuel and Stella Harrison," Dionne stated.

I giggled at her statement, flipped the burgers over, and pulled the fries out to let them sit.

"The famous Harrison family that owns about half the town," I recalled as I picked up a French fry to eat. Once everything was finished, I filled their plates, split the burger in half with fries, and placed it in front of them. "Here you go, fellas. Don't fight please." I bent down to kiss their foreheads, then made myself a plate.

"Yeah, from what I remember, Stella acts like she's the queen of North Park," Dionne mentioned. Her mind was always drifting off to how she wouldn't let anyone bully her friends or family. Whatever Stella has done to Dionne or people she loves will never leave her brain.

I listened to her ramble on and on about Stella and her family. "Dionne, thanks for checking in with me. We're good and eating dinner now." I picked up the napkin to wipe the ketchup off my lip. The thought of Khalil being related to Stella meant he probably had the same uppity attitude.

"All right, how are you getting the boys to school in the morning and then to work?" Dionne checked.

I watched Silas push his burger around his plate, playing with the ketchup. I wiggled a finger at him to eat. "I was going to call a cab or Uber." I gulped my drink.

"I can pick you guys up," Dionne offered.

"You don't have to do that." My problems are my own and unconvincingly my friends weighed heavy on me. They knew my issues from moving and dealing with Jaylen.

"Those are my babies. I won't take no for an answer," Dionne commented.

The distant sounds of the TV playing old Scooby Doo filled my ears.

I tossed another fry in my mouth. "Thanks, Dionne. I appreciate you." I smiled and hung up.

"Mommy, this is good," Prince praised with a wide grin.

"Thank you, baby. Now finish eating so you can get ready for your baths and go to bed." We chatted for the next hour and laughed. I helped the boys bathe, got them tucked away in bed, and I cleaned up the kitchen. I finally had a moment for myself to breathe and relax in a bubble bath with a glass of wine.

2
______

SERENA

The next morning, I ran around getting the boys dressed along with myself since I overslept. Dionne would be here in ten minutes, and she was always on time whenever she needed to take the boys to school. I heard the doorbell ring, and I slid Silas into his shirt while he ate his bowl of cereal. I turned to brush over Prince's hair and ran to open the door for Dionne.

"Good morning," Dionne cheerfully said and hugged me.

All around me chaos erupted and I was ready to call out and go back to bed. "We're almost ready. You want some coffee?" I inquired as I released her, ran to the bedroom, and grabbed my shoes. I had to be at Savory for a few hours, then work on my cupcake business. I loved baking; it was one of my passions that I fell in love with before the boys were born. I'd always had plans of starting my own business and hoped to have support from family and friends, but things didn't work out that way.

"I'll take a little. Go finish getting ready. I'll watch the boys," Dionne answered, walking in the kitchen.

"Auntie Dionne!" Silas and Prince yelled.

I heard laughter and joking from the kitchen as I finished putting on my shoes and grabbed the brush to put my hair into a ponytail. I grabbed my purse, keys, jacket, and cell phone before heading back into the kitchen to get things cleaned up. I noticed Dionne already had the boys lined up at the door with their coats on and lunch boxes in hand.

"You cleaned up the kitchen?" I scanned the area, pointing to the washed dishes and the cleaned table.

"I have some skills; I just may not display them all. But I'm a little clean freak at home," Dionne mentioned.

"Thanks. Let me grab their car seats, and we can go." I lifted them from the corner of the room.

Dionne rubbed the top of their heads. "Boys, are you ready for a beautiful day?" Dionne pulled them close.

"Yes, ma'am," they both replied, not sounding like my crazy toddlers that keep me up all day and night.

"Don't look shocked; they just like me better," Dionne teased as the boys walked out of the apartment and behaved during the walk toward her car.

The only time I saw them acting so sweet and calm was with my parents because they spoiled them rotten. I could sometimes get them to behave, but it was still a huge negotiation. I helped buckle in the boys and jumped in on the passenger side of the car.

"What are you going to do about your car?" Dionne queried, as she backed out of my driveway and headed to the stop sign at the end of the street. I saw Harmony outside, and I waved.

"Hopefully, Arvon will let me know today." I typed a note in my phone to remind myself to call Arvon on my break. The scenery passing by was baffling compared to yesterday and the crazy rain.

"You need a new car, girl. It's so old, and this isn't the first time it's broken down," Dionne reminded me.

I groaned in annoyance, not ready to hear another person tell me how I needed a new car like I could make it pop up out of the blue. The amount of responsibilities I had right now topped getting a new car.

I arched an eyebrow, shrugging. "Well, with the imaginary money I have, I'll get on that."

"Ohh, don't get snappy with me, honey. You can always ask your parents or your ex." Dionne adjusted her seat.

I looked at her like she had grown two heads. "I refuse to take a handout from anyone."

"I refuse to take a handout... blah... blah... blah," Dionne repeated, turning the radio on.

I glanced in the backseat to see if the boys were listening, but they were on the iPad game Dionne bought for them to use whenever she had them in her car.

Dionne tapped me on the shoulder. "He owes you for taking care of his kids," Dionne commented.

"I know, Dionne. Can we change the subject please? I'd rather discuss something else," I groaned, picking the lint off my shirt.

Dionne pulled up to the restaurant and put the car in park.

I raised my hand to unlock the door. "Are you good with taking them into school? I hate to put more work on you."

"I'll be fine. Plus, I have Prince in my class, so it works out perfectly." Dionne turned to face the boys and smiled.

"Thanks, Dionne. I'll be over to pick them up afterwards." I got out of the car and walked to the backseat. As I kissed them both on the forehead, I made them promise to be good. "Be good for Dionne, okay?" I lifted Prince and Silas by the chin to look into my eyes.

"We promise," they both spoke, grinning and showing pearly white teeth.

I didn't know if it was a good thing to leave them with Dionne or not; they could get anything out of her when they were alone. One time I came over, they had a swimming pool in the backyard of Dionne's place. Her boyfriend Amos was fine with the boys hanging around since he wanted to practice for when they had kids, even though Dionne said she wasn't ready for that big of a commitment.

When I went inside the restaurant, I saw Wasim sitting at the bar with paperwork in front of him. Normally, when things were busy early in the morning, he came out of the office to hang with the staff while we set up for the day. I walked up to the barstool next to him.

"Hey, Wasim," I greeted him, removed my jacket, and prepared to go in the back to set up for my shift.

"Did I just see you get dropped off?" Wasim slid the papers together in his file folder.

I held everything in my hands. "Yeah, my car broke down yesterday after I picked up the boys."

"Thank God you're here," Eboan rushed, coming over to hug me.

I glanced at my watch to see if I was running late. "What are you being dramatic about?" I teased, releasing from his hug.

"He has a party to cater in a half hour for six women," Wasim mentioned.

"Let me guess. You need my help?" I hinted as I poked Eboan with my hip.

"Yes, please, and they requested a fresh batch of

cupcakes to take home," Eboan begged, poking his lip out, with both hands in prayer.

I groaned in frustration. I didn't like people requesting cupcakes from me without prior notice. Now, I'd have to figure out a plan to bake some in a short amount of time and lose money from waitressing.

"Eboan, you know I like prior notice about orders," I fussed, then walked off toward the employee door to hang up my coat and slide my purse in our locker.

Eboan followed me and hung his arm around my shoulder. "This was a last-minute call; don't be mad. They wanted the lemon tart cupcakes," he replied like it was simple to whip up a dozen cupcakes to have fresh and ready. Eboan had worked at Savory for years, and we quickly became the best of friends, along with Dionne, Nori, and Arvon. I felt a newfound freedom living here in North Park.

"Don't be mad," I mocked him and grabbed my apron from the locker, tying it around my waist. I headed into the kitchen and greeted the staff with morning hellos and hugs. It was a full family at Savory. Sometimes I never wanted to leave, but my goal was to start my own cupcake business one day. My parents thought I had made a big mistake skipping college and ending up pregnant by Jaylen when I was twenty-one. We struggled for a while as he worked full-time in construction, but he actually spent most of his money on women and gambling. The biggest issue in our relationship was his inability to keep his dick in his pants, which had every woman fawning all over him. It started after he hurt himself playing college ball, from which he never fully recovered. That's when I came into the picture. He catered to me and made me feel like I was the most important person in his life. At the time, I thought we were building something, until I got pregnant, and he felt I was holding him back. All the late-night phone calls and messages became too much for me. I couldn't stay in the relationship any longer. So, I left and moved in with my parents, but even then, I wasn't completely free from judgement.

I pointed at him with a towel in my hand. "I'll make them this one time, but you owe me." I wiped the counter and faced Eboan.

"You're the best. Let me know if you need anything." Eboan pressed a hand on my shoulder.

I grabbed the empty bowls and picked up the carton of eggs and a gallon of milk from the fridge. I then picked up the sugar, lemon juice, and oil spray, and prepared the oven. Fifteen minutes later, the kitchen was full of staff running in and out, calling out orders.

"I need an order of French toast!" Uliana yelled.

"Not before my fried eggs and pancakes," Maahir demanded.

I tossed the empty carton of eggs in the trash. "Is it busy out there already?" I wiped my hands on my apron and swiped my forehead with the back of my hand.

"Yep. Are you making that for the boys?" Maahir chuckled, handing a plate toward another waitress. Moving around I pulled more tickets up to get started on.

I shook my head. "No." I prepared to decorate the cupcakes once they were done. I liked to put my special spin and add a little rum when adults requested the cupcakes, but I wasn't sure if it was all adults today. Since this was a last-minute order, I went with the normal recipe until I could get time to plan out my next batch. Eboan walked into the kitchen with a notepad and tray, picking up the glasses of water.

I puffed air through my lungs. "Is the group party here?" I darted eyes toward Eboan.

"I'm annoyed already with their requests," Eboan grunted. He sounded frustrated as he wiped the sweat off his forehead.

"Let me guess. They didn't stick to the approved list of items they could order in a party?" I questioned as I swung my head back to icing cupcakes.

"No they did not, and the woman who set this up is already doing too much," he huffed as he filled the rest of the glasses with water.

"Let me help. I'm done with the cupcakes; they just need to cool off." I picked up the second tray and helped grab the drink orders. Eboan put the food order in, and I followed with a tray of drinks for six people. The front of the restaurant was booming early with people laughing and talking as the sound of the cash register rang up some of the regular customers in line. I waved at Mr. Joe and Catherine, an older couple who came in every morning for breakfast.

"Ladies, I have your water and drinks. This is Serena, and she'll be helping me," Eboan mentioned me, and I smiled. All the women were dressed in colorful sundresses and white hats. They ranged in age from late twenties to early fifties.

"Mother Stella, are you sure about this plan?" the younger one said as she put the straw in the glass and took a sip. She was all dolled up with her hair pinned to the back in a tight bun. Her chestnut, golden-brown skin was blocked out by the overdramatic makeup and long lashes that looked like her eyes were heavy and ready to tip over. She snapped her fingers for Eboan, and I could tell he was getting ready to burst.

"Hi. I'm Serena, what can I help you with?" I placed another drink down in front of the woman sitting to her right side.

"I need more ice." She pasted on a smile.

"Lexi, this will work. Let me handle the invites," the older woman named Stella sitting at the head of the table stated.

I tossed her a look. "Sure, I'll get that for you." I picked up her glass and watched as they giggled in laughter from an inside joke. "Eboan, I'm going to check on the food," I called out as I went to the kitchen. I blew out a breath to gather myself before going back to the table.

His shoulders slumped. "Those are some crazy women," Eboan said, shaking his head and grabbing the plates of food to take back out there.

"Yeah, they're a piece of work," I muttered.

Uliana burst through the door with Wasim right behind her.

"Eboan, make sure Stella's ticket is taken care of because they're ordering off the menu," Wasim spoke as he headed to his office.

"Eboan, after this, I have to work on my tables before it's time to pick up the boys," I said as I gathered the last two plates off the counter and walked out to the party table.

Stella stood and walked around the table, passing out small boxes.

I spoke in a gentle tone. "Here's your drink with more ice, and I have two orders of scramblers," I said to the crowd, there was a heavy feeling in my stomach.

The Lexi girl sipped her drink and ignored my comment about the plates of food. I rolled my eyes, continued on, and set the second plate down. I walked away to my section and spoke with two guests who wanted only coffee for right now. I took the orders down of just bacon, toast, and eggs. By early afternoon, I was finished with my shift. I closed out my tickets and replaced the pastries in the front display. I cleaned up my section and talked with Uliana and Maahir about the rest of the day.

"Excuse me... Hello!" I heard and turned to see Stella standing at the door of the employee entrance.

I narrowed my eyes, moving closer to her. "I'm sorry, you can't come back here."

"Who are you?" she spat, eyebrows going skyward.

"What can I help you with?" I released a drawn-out exhale, pulling extra menus up from the back counter and walking to the hostess area. I planted back in place, she moved toward the employee door.

Stella crossed her arms, tapping her feet. "I need more of those cupcakes. My husband would love them," she said.

"Unfortunately, we're all out of them. Check back at the end of the week," I replied.

Stella dropped her hands. "What do you mean you're out of cupcakes?" she huffed.

"I'm the one who makes them, and I wasn't informed of your original order, so this was a last-minute thing."

She motioned to the back. "Okay, so can you go and make them before we leave?" Stella was irritated at me.

I was becoming more anxious being alone with her. "Sorry, I'm done with my shift now," I answered.

Stella gasped. "Do you know who I am?" Stella planted her hand on her hip, her lip turning in a scowl.

"Actually, I don't, and I need to leave because my ride is here. Eboan can help you further though." I walked into the employee area to get my jacket and purse. The tension was growing and I knew it would lead to me being in trouble because of her last name. I pulled my phone out to call an Uber, lying about my ride already being here and headed up to the boys' school.

3

SERENA

I pulled up to the school in a car ride and hopped out as the bell rang. I headed inside as the kids crowded the hallways, waving at the boys as they stood with Nori and Dionne at the front of her classroom.

"Hi, boys." I was determined to let the situation go and put on a nice smile for my kids, bending down to hug them and kiss their cheeks, then stood to grab their bookbags.

"Dionne told me your car is at the shop with Arvon?" Nori inquired as Horace walked out of her classroom. Prince whispered something in his ear.

I learned my best friends are very involved in knowing every detail if something happens to me. I loved that about them, but right now the idea of going down the previous day's events and feeling like I will explode any minute from interaction with Stella caused me to remember the boys were here and they could see when my energy changes. "Yeah, it was towed to his shop yesterday. I took an Uber up here, all good though."

"If we didn't have a teacher's meeting, I could have taken

you home." Dionne waved at another student leaving her room.

"Hi, Kayla!" Silas yelled out behind me.

A little girl's voice wafted in the air. "Hi, Silas!" Kayla shouted back.

"Kayla, what did I say about all that yelling?" he voiced, challenging her to reply.

I tensed up at the familiar deep, raspy voice.

Silas released Kayla. "Mommy, you remember the man from the rain," Silas said, tapping my leg.

I became instantly stuck in place. "Silas, stop pointing," I commanded and nudged his hand down.

Dionne smirked at me, then winked with a mischievous plan in her eye. "Hi, Khalil," Dionne spoke, waving her hand.

I tugged lowly on her shirt. "Dionne, you're embarrassing yourself," I whispered in her ear.

"Hey, Nori. What's up, Dionne?" Khalil cocked his head, moving in closer.

I heard Khalil say behind me, a chill ran over me.

A little girl popped up beside me and passed a sheet of paper to Silas. I assumed that was his daughter Silas was speaking to. There's nothing worse than running into the person that has the same last name as the woman that just gave you hell a few minutes ago. I was honestly shocked he was related to her from the way she acted and how he was pleasant to help us yesterday.

He wrapped arm around Kayla's shoulder.

"Hey, Khalil. Have you met Serena yet?" Nori asked.

Khalil stepped forward and cast a glance over at me with a smirk on his face, showcasing his steely jawline and perfect full lips. "We met already. She was the car I had towed to Arvon's the other night," Khalil reminded us all.

Dionne bumped me on the shoulder. "Isn't this a coincidence? Serena still is without a car, and she was planning to take a car service home. Since you're here, maybe you can take her home." Dionne pushed me forward.

I opened and closed mouth, waving my hand in the air. "No," I hurriedly said.

Dionne held a deadpan look, lip twisted up. "Why not? He's probably going your way!" Dionne mentioned.

I cleared my throat. "He's not," I answered, grabbing the bookbags before they fell off my arm.

Khalil titled his chin down, sneering at me. "He can speak for himself," Khalil stated, holding his daughter's hand.

"Are you sure, Khalil? If we didn't have this meeting, I would have offered," Nori said as she ran a hand across Silas' head.

Nori could tell I wanted to crawl into a hole right now from Dionne pushing him. Right now was not the time to curse my friend out, but I would speak on her trying to run my life.

Khalil lifted Kayla's bag up. "It's no problem. I see Kayla already vouched for them," Khalil told her.

His eyes sent a private message to me.

I brushed a palm down my face. "You don't have to do this. Your daughter is probably tired and ready to go home." I tried to suppress the awkwardness of the moment.

"My niece is fine, and we had plans to stop for ice cream anyway," Khalil informed me, and all the kids jumped up and down and screamed.

Prince clapped hands with his brother. "Ice cream! Yay! Mommy, can we get ice cream too?" Prince suggested.

"No, and you know better," I scolded.

Khalil eyed me up and down. "Are you always this

uptight?" Khalil asked before he walked off with Kayla beside him.

Silas and Prince slid out of my hands and walked with Khalil and his niece, shocking me.

I planted both hands on top of my head. "What just happened?" I whispered aloud, catching the mocking, agitated tone in his words.

"Uhm... I think you just met Khalil Harrison," Dionne joked.

I flipped her off before I rushed down the hall to the boys. "Silas and Prince, you know better than running away from me." I grasped their hands before they wandered away.

"Hi, I'm Kayla." Kayla held out her hand for me to shake.

I smiled and captured her tiny palm. "Hi, Kayla. I'm Serena." I ignored the heated stare from Khalil.

She turned to hand him her little lunch box.

Khalil dropped down to face level with the kids. "Boys, what's your favorite ice cream?" he asked.

"I like chocolate." Silas hugged himself.

"I like vanilla," Prince mentioned.

"What about your mom?" Khalil questioned, pointing at me.

His presence had an indefinable feeling of rightness and that meant it would only lead to heartbreak for my boys and me. I can't have them hurt again.

Silas put his little finger to his chin in thought. "Mommy likes chocolate, vanilla, and strawberry," Silas told all my business.

Khalil cocked his head, staring at me while talking to the boys. "Is that right?" Khalil questioned, licking his lips, showing no sign of relenting.

It felt like the two of us were having a conversation that no one else knew. I shook myself out of the moment, ushering them forward to leave so we can try and catch a ride home.

I ambled them down the walkway. "Okay, we need to get going. It's nice meeting you, Kayla."

"I'll drop you off right after ice cream," Khalil stated as he turned the alarm off in his car and opened the door for the kids.

The cynicism of the remark grated on me. Everyone around me thought they knew what was best for me.

"You're not taking us home again." I tried weighing the whole structure of events within the last twenty-four hours.

Khail's glare burned through me. "Get in the car," Khalil demanded and pinched the top of his nose.

"No, Mr. Harrison." My pride canceled my inner turmoil. What if his family finds out it was me that had the situation with Stella, what if the boys get attached and he's doing all of this because he thinks we're charity. What if I actually like him and he sees a woman that's not on his level.

All three of the kids looked between us as I stood with my arms crossed, and Khalil stood next to the car door, waiting for me to get inside.

"We had this discussion about you being stubborn already. It's just a ride," Khalil stated, tapping his hand on the door.

My mind refused to register the significance of his words.

"This is the last time. No more rides, Mr. Harrison." It was impossible to steady my erratic pulse when he was near. Up close I took in his smooth skin, the cute shape of his ears, and the strong scent that had me clenching my thighs tight.

"Khalil," he said, voice uncompromising.

I jerked the door open and paused. "What?" I pressed.

"Call me Khalil, Serena." He helped the kids get in the car and turned the video monitor on in the backseat for them.

His tone was velvet yet edged with steel.

Dionne is going to hear about this.

I grasped my phone to text her. "So, Kayla's your niece?" I queried, sparking up conversation.

> **Me:** *I hope you get the bubble guts from dairy.*
> **Dionne:** *Lol! Bestie are you enjoying your date?*

I grunted, typing back.

> **Me:** *This is not a date and you will pay.*
> **Dionne:** *I think you two look good together.*

"Yeah, my brother's daughter," Khalil replied as he turned into traffic toward the ice cream shop down the street from Zymir's tattoo shop Inked.

I ignored her reply and closed out of the thread.

"Do you have any kids?" I probed.

"Would it matter?" He drove down the street and parked in an open space in front of Sweet Bliss' Treats, that also served as a hangout spot like Savory. He turned the car off as the kids cheered in joy and faced me.

We held each other's stare before I faced the kids.

I jumped out of the car next. "Kayla, you want to show the boys your favorite flavor?" I had to fight to keep my personal thoughts together and focus on the kids.

Khalil held the front door open for them as they got in line.

I chuckled as they sang.

"Ice cream, we all scream for ice cream."

"Silas, you both will only get one scoop. I still need to make dinner," I said, pointing between him and Prince.

Silas clapped his hands on the window of the ice cream display. "Ahhhh Mom..." Silas whined.

The cashier giggled at them.

"Listen to your mom, little man. You don't want to get too full of ice cream," Khalil agreed and winked at me when Silas peered up at him.

"You're right. Thanks, Khalil," Silas answered without a fuss.

My mouth hung wide open at how agreeable they were being with him compared to when I had them. They went at each other's throats over the smallest things and were in constant competition for my attention. Their father could barely discipline them without screaming and yelling, and here was this stranger calmly telling them to listen to me.

"Hi, welcome to Sweet Bliss' Treats. What can I get for you?" the cashier questioned.

Kayla and Prince called out for chocolate.

"Let's get two chocolates, strawberry, and for you?" Khalil motioned at me and pulled his wallet out to pay.

"I'm fine, and I can pay for the boys' ice cream." I started to go into my purse.

Khalil stopped me with his hand. "My treat," Khalil explained as he took out a fifty-dollar bill and paid.

I felt an instant rise in my anxiety. "I don't need you paying for them and having me owe you."

"I know that. Did I say you owed me anything?" Khalil asked me, closing the space between us.

Every time his gaze met mine, my heart turned over in response.

The cashier tried to pass him his change, and he waved her off. We stared into each other's eyes, and I felt something I hadn't felt in a long time for a man. His eyes seemed to be a mirror into his soul, like he wanted to offer protection. Also, something in his nature gave off a vibe not to question him because I'd be going back and forth for hours. I saw the low smirk at the corner of his mouth and full lips that begged to be a distraction I didn't need in my life. I cleared my throat and stepped back to put space between us.

"Let me help you, Prince," I told my son, to keep him from spilling anything on his clothes.

He reached up on the counter to grab the scoop of ice cream. I grabbed a stack of napkins and picked up the tray. All three kids walked to the table in the back corner of the shop and sat. Prince, Kayla, and Silas sat in the booth together. That left Khalil and me on the other side.

I looked over as Khalil pulled his vibrating phone out of his pocket, smiled, and returned a text. I knew something about that smile had to do with a woman, so I needed to get myself in check. He would never look at me in that way. Being a mother of two kids and working a nine-to-three job with a host of issues, a crazy ex-boyfriend, and parents who still thought I was a child was enough to deal with without adding a man to the equation.

"Mommy, can Kayla come to dinner?" Prince ignored the ice cream mustache he had on his face.

I chuckled, picking up the napkin to clean it away. "Sweetie, not tonight." I debated on the amount of budgeting I had to do for school shopping in a few weeks.

"Please, can I, Uncle Khalil?" Kayla begged.

"Not tonight, Kayla," Khalil stated as he continued to text.

Silas poked out his lip. "Why not?" Silas questioned as he scooped up more ice cream on his spoon.

I wiped his mouth clear of any excess, then started on his sticky hands.

"Yeah, why not?" Kayla questioned.

Seemed like a gang up and we were getting bullied by children.

"He has a date tonight. We can't interfere with that," I chortled.

Khalil turned toward me, placed his phone down, and leaned back in the booth with his arm around the back, giving us his undivided attention. "Actually, I have work that needs to be handled, and Kayla has dance class after this."

"Oh, I forgot about that," Kayla agreed, and sat back in her seat.

"Yeah, you forgot about that. You begged your dad to enroll you," Khalil stated, while looking at me.

Kayla glanced between us. "Can they come to our house for dinner?" Kayla continued.

"Yay!" Silas and Prince yelled at the same time.

I rubbed both hands on my thighs. "Sorry, not tonight, Kayla. I have too much work tonight."

Khalil hands clasped together and he leaned forward. "What about dinner tomorrow?" Khalil inquired.

"Huh." I was confused by his unexpected question, close to not having anymore interactions between us and here he goes again.

"If you can huh, you can hear," Khalil bluntly stated.

Kayla grinned. "We can have my favorite pasta that Jessica makes." Kayla passed some ice cream over to Silas.

I gulped down a response, lowering my gaze to check my watch. "Look at the time. Come on, boys. Hurry up so we can get you home, and I can start cooking."

"Do I make you nervous, Serena?" Khalil whispered, leaning close to my ear.

I felt a shiver from the brush of his leg against mine. "No. I just need to make sure my car is working."

The very air around us seemed electrified.

"I can have a car pick you up," Khalil informed me.

"I'll think about it." I motioned for him to let me out of the booth. I tossed Prince and Silas' trash away.

Khalil stood, pushed his left hand in his pocket, and grabbed Kayla's hand to hold the door open for everyone to leave. Everyone piled inside and got comfortable like it was a normal thing as a family outing. The kids laughed and joked in the backseat while I hummed low to the music on the radio and focused on the drive back home.

Thirty minutes later, we pulled up to my place. Khalil helped the kids out of the backseat, then walked around to assist me as I grabbed their things, and he followed us to the door.

I dropped the bags and turned toward him with the door halfway open. "Thanks again for the ride," I thanked him, mentally preparing myself to block out him from my memory.

Khalil leaned against the door, with his arms hovered above me. "You're welcome," he responded.

His appeal was devastating.

I looked everywhere but at him. "I'll let you know about dinner tomorrow."

"You do that," he replied as he glanced down at my lips, then back to my eyes.

"I didn't get a chance to pay you back yesterday." I spoke right as his phone vibrated again.

He removed it from his pocket. "I need to take this," Khalil stated as he answered right in front of me and grabbed my hand to stop me from leaving.

"I can—"

He held a finger up to give him a moment. "What's up, Foster?" Khalil looked over at Kayla sitting in the front seat, playing with her doll. "I'll see you in the morning. Call a meeting," Khalil commented then hung up.

"Business." I tried to remove my hand.

He tightened his grip. "Always. I need to get her home to my brother, so she can get to class," Khalil responded. He lifted my hand gently and ran his palm across it.

"Of course, and I need to get these boys fed and off to bed." I giggled, tapping my nails on the doorknob. The boys ran in front of the TV to replay the *Justice League* movie.

"Eight tomorrow night," Khalil told me, walking backwards toward his car, grinning.

"Tomorrow." I enjoyed the gentle sparring as much as he did.

I closed the door and watched him reverse out as Kayla laughed and held up her doll in his face.

"Momma, can we have chicken tonight?" Prince asked, pushing his toy fire truck around Silas as he watched the movie.

I picked up Prince to kiss the side of his cheek and tickle him, then placed him back down on the floor. "I will make baked chicken, brown rice, and broccoli."

"Yuck, broccoli," Prince repeated.

I laughed, then walked into the kitchen to start dinner. The house phone rang, and I picked it up to see my mom calling. "Hello." I shoved my purse on the counter.

"You're home," Mom spoke.

"We are," I responded, looking into the living room at the kids laughing.

"Your father wanted the kids to come over this weekend," Mom demanded.

When Clara and Roman Dunn put in a request, they

expected me to give in. This one time, I might not fight them on sending the boys over since I needed to get caught up on business. I set up a few walk throughs of spaces this weekend to see what the cost would be to rent. I had a little savings and hoped to one day have enough to set up the first six months of bills.

I picked up the saucepans from the bottom cabinet. "Sure, Mom."

"Okay, how's work going?" she questioned.

I pushed the phone between my neck and shoulder, washing my hands. "Work is fine. The restaurant is busy, and I'm planning some new recipes."

"Have you spoken with Jaylen? Your father talked with him a week ago," Mom blurted out.

I sighed and paused my next words before I said something I might regret. "I don't care what Jaylen is talking about, Mom." I grabbed the food from the fridge and started separating things to prepare.

"Serena, it's not always about you and your feelings," Mom fussed.

"Mommy I want some water!" Silas yelled.

I seasoned the chicken and placed it in the oven as Silas ran into the kitchen. I caught the note of edge in her response.

"Silas, only a little bit. Dinner will be ready soon." I picked up a glass and pushed it under the cupholder of the fridge to dispense water. I handed it to Silas and went back to dinner. "Ma, don't start. If Jaylen wants to see his kids, he can call me to make arrangements," I said, stirring the rice.

"Serena, you continue to live in a foolish state of thinking a man is just going to fall at your feet." Mom's tone had become chilly.

"No, I don't want a man to fall at my feet. I'm good with

just me and the boys." I felt a strange comfort in finally sticking up to her as my phone beeped with an incoming call.

"He wants to get back together, and I think it's a good idea," Mom called out.

I turned the rice down low and wiped the counter down. "I have another call. I have to go."

"Serena," Mom hissed.

I bit my lip to stifle a groan. "Mom, no, I need to get this call," I said, clicking over to the other call.

"How did it go?" Dionne asked.

"How did what go?" I pulled some plates from the cabinet and set the table for dinner. I headed to my bedroom to change into more comfortable clothes now that things had calmed down. I heard rustling on the other end of the phone.

"Khalil and you with the kids," Dionne nosily butted in on my life.

I shuffled to the nightstand removing my jewelry. "Nothing to tell, Dionne. I'm not looking for a man." Then I stepped out of my clothes, keeping the door slightly ajar to listen to the kids.

"Nothing wrong with having a friend," Dionne teased. I heard voices talking in the background.

I laughed at her statement and opened the drawer to grab a shirt and shorts. "I have you as a friend, Nori, and my kids."

"That doesn't count. You need a grown-up of the opposite sex type of friend," Dionne tittered, cursing at someone on the other end.

I blew out a breath, hearing the beep of the other line. "Dionne, I have my mom on the other end."

"Tell her I said hi, but this is an emergency."

I tossed my hand up exasperated at everyone bugging me at the same time. "Dionne get off my phone."

"Fine, but tell me did you kiss?"

I burst into laughter listening to her and stepped back in the kitchen after changing and chuckled at her going on and on about my lack of a love life and the teachers' meeting she had today. She asked if I wanted to go out for drinks tomorrow night with a few friends. I agreed since it had been a while for me to have a night out without the boys and this helped me to avoid Khalil's invitation all together.

"Dionne, I'm about to have dinner with the boys," I said.

"Fine, just think about what I said and give the boys a kiss from me," Dionne told me, and we ended our call. I told the boys to come into the kitchen to eat. We talked about their day and what they had coming up before getting ready for bed and school tomorrow. I tucked them both in their bunk beds and kissed the top of their foreheads. After turning the light out and closing the door, I went into the bathroom and showered. I fell into bed thinking about the next time I might see Khalil.

4

KHALIL

I was still thinking about the first time I had met Serena and her two boys on the freeway when her car broke down. Then taking them out for ice cream with Kayla. I smirked, glancing out the window at the moving traffic. I was close to driving past her car, but something kept nudging at me to stop and help. Normally, when I had business to handle, I stuck to my schedule, but this one time, I deviated from my routine and ended up meeting the most beautiful woman I had ever met. She had the most warm, rich, dark-brown skin with a small nose and full lips that I tried many times not to think about throughout the day. Serena was short as hell compared to my six-two height, probably coming up to my chest. She had to be about five-six or seven with thick curves underneath her uniform that she tried to hide, but I could see the weight from her two boys left her with a round ass, thick hips, and an hourglass figure. I noticed when she was unsure about something or conflicted, her eyebrows would bunch up together to come up with an excuse to say no. Serena would make someone a great wife one day, and I'd be jealous of the man who had the pleasure of waking up to a calm spirit like hers.

A perfect stranger had already crept into my head and caused me to want to explore the idea of dating and possibly becoming more. I prided myself on never getting married and having kids, but just the thought of Silas and Prince had me rethinking my goals for the future. I took a look at my watch then looked out my office window to prepare the words for this meeting. Growing up as Samuel and Stella Harrison's younger son, I needed to be in line with the vision they set out for me. That was to run for future office and ingrain our family in the establishment that would have lifelong leverage. My grandfather was the mayor, my great-grandfather was the governor, and my dad was currently the mayor. He wanted me to run behind him. I loved working for myself in my investment firm. I'd always had an eye for finding companies that needed restructuring and funding to mold into a bigger idea than what it started out as. I was currently on the verge of becoming the youngest owner of a three-hundred-million-dollar conglomerate.

My mother Stella was a stay-at-home mom and wife who ran the household and oversaw the Harrison Charity Foundation. I had an older brother Kendall, who was thirty-three and had his own construction business, a wife, and his daughter Kayla. We were planning his upcoming birthday next month, and my mom wanted to have a huge family dinner to announce me running for office. At twenty-nine and single, putting my life out for the public to judge, wasn't the type of thing I needed at the moment. She tried her best to push me and Lexi Jeffries back together. We had dated in high school, then college. The Harrison and Jeffries families had a long history between us that could basically create the ultimate political dynasty if Lexi and I got married and had children.

I knew Serena thought I was texting another woman at the ice cream shop, but it was my mom sending me ideas for my brother's party and wanting to use Savory as the location with the cake being done by someone who made her favorite lemon cupcakes or some shit.

"They're ready, sir," my assistant Antoine said, holding the office door open.

"Did you get the report finished like I asked?" I inquired, reaching out for the documents Antoine researched on the next building I was thinking of buying.

"Yes, sir. I have the notes from the inspector and plumbing company," Antoine told me.

"Great, let's do this," I replied. I flipped through the documents as we walked from my office to the conference room. Harrison and Associates could be your best friend or worst enemy as a company if you didn't have all your ducks in a row. This online company was up for sale, and they'd tried to stronghold me out of a bidding war. I wasn't waiting any longer. I opened the door of the conference room and noticed their lawyer sitting there today. They must have felt it would go the way they wanted.

"Larry, nice to see you again," I said, extending a hand for a shake.

"Hello, Mr. Harrison," Larry said, sweat coasting down his forehead.

"Please call me Khalil. My dad is Mr. Harrison." I unbuttoned my jacket and sat in the chair at the head of the conference table.

Larry adjusted his tie, nervously. "Khalil, I'm glad we could meet again," Larry stated.

I reached over for the glass and poured some water,

slowly taking in his nervousness and hesitation. "Sure about that?" I questioned, training my gaze on him.

"My client wants to make sure everything is correct with his vision for his company." Larry's lawyer's vexation was evident.

"His company," I spoke and opened the file folder. The Harrison name is prominent in business and learning from the best allowed me to see the various degrees of how to read a person.

He gritted his teeth. "Khalil, we both know how much my company is worth, and I thought you saw the vision as well," Larry implied, soured with frustration.

"I do know the worth, and that's why I'm giving you the courtesy of taking my last final offer," I said, reminding myself of my being humble, but with an enormous, positive ego.

"Which is?" Larry's expression clouded in anger.

I sat back in my chair, clasping my hands together. "Two million, and that's me being generous," I insisted.

Larry's dark snappy eyes shifted from his lawyer to me. "That's bullshit, Khalil. Your last offer was ten million." Larry jumped up in shock.

"Larry, calm down," Tom chastised him.

He immediately sat back down. "Hell no, he can't drop the amount like that!" Larry shouted, his chest rose and fell.

I grinned, watching him explode. "Actually, Larry, I can, and I did. Your company has taken on so much debt, the banks are calling me in good faith to try to get their money back. As you know, being the son of the mayor, I can get enough information to know exactly what I would be investing my money behind. At first, I had plans to keep you with the company."

"That's a lie!" Larry screamed, balling his fist up ready to fight.

I cocked my head to the side, amused at him thinking he could beat my ass. "So, you're not in debt up to fifteen million? Employees have reported an unstable work environment. Shall I go on?" I inquired.

"What are the stipulations of the deal, Mr. Harrison?" Tom quizzed.

I sat forward. "I'm glad you asked, Tom."

"I'm not selling," Larry grunted out, frown lines creasing.

"Two million that will be allocated to you at one point five and the rest toward your employees who want to leave without issue. The rest, if they want to stay, can. You are no longer attached to the company."

A muscle beat in his jaw. "Can he do this?" Larry asked his attorney.

"The amount of media attention on your company and debt would have you in litigation for years," I advised, ready to wrap up the conversation and move on with my day.

"I think it's a fair offer, Larry." Tom tapped the pen on the table and Antoine handed the paperwork over to him to sign.

There's nothing worse than seeing your dreams falter, but Larry wanted to be rich without the solid reality of work it entails. He'd forgotten the discipline and structure to forecast how things would end up.

"I built this company from the ground up, and you're just going to take it away," Larry complained.

"I'm saving the company from being destroyed and giving you a chance at a clean slate."

Once Larry got over the initial shock, he signed the paperwork and left with his lawyer. I sat back in the chair and thought of the ways in which I could celebrate this big win tonight, then I remembered I had dinner plans with Serena and the kids.

"Mr. Harrison, did you know your father is on the line for you?" Antonine mentioned, holding the phone line out for me to take.

I stood at the door. "Thanks, can you get the contract over to accounting and our lawyer?"

"Yes, sir. Are you having the usual for lunch?" Antoine asked.

"I'm heading to Savory for lunch." I piled up the papers and handed them to him.

Antoine strolled beside me down the hall. "Sounds good," Antoine said.

"Yeah," I spoke into the phone.

"Is that the way you address your father?" my dad asked.

I blew out a breath in annoyance. "Father."

"Khalil, don't get too high and mighty, boy," Dad argued.

"What can I do for you?" I groaned, scratching the back of my neck. I scanned the time and saw it was going on ten a.m. Usually, he had press conferences during this time.

"I wanted to make sure you're thinking about what we discussed," Dad told me.

"I haven't made up my mind yet."

"Son, your place is here with the family. Nothing wrong with still having your business on the side. Since your brother has decided to not follow in the family tradition, we have our hopes with you," Dad pushed.

"You mean stronghold me into taking on the family tradition."

I heard him chuckle on the other end of the call.

"Why are you so against the Harrison name? Growing up, you used it to your advantage," Dad remarked.

"I was a kid, and kids do dumb shit. I don't love Lexi, and I don't care about politics."

"But you care about money, right?" Dad brought up again.

"Shouldn't you be recruiting some sucker to do this job? Every decision will be questioned and put upon by your people," I spat, feeling myself get frustrated.

"This is about legacy, Khalil, and our family joining with the Jeffries!" Dad yelled.

"No, this is about you and Michael Jeffries forming some alliance to control the people of North Park."

"So, do you think you've made all that money on your own? I can tell you what the Harrison name has done for you," Dad hinted, getting under my skin.

"Kendall was right about you. Always throwing stuff in people's faces," I said, then ended the call without letting him comment. This was the shit I didn't like about family; anytime I thought my father was doing something in good faith, it came with an agenda. Basically, he put me in debt to him, and I refused to be a pawn in his political game. Michael Jeffries was the lieutenant governor and in line for the top governor position in a few months. My dad planned to run for lieutenant governor and have me run for mayor, keeping everything under Harrison and Jeffries control. If Lexi and I married, that was an even bigger piece of the political pie; they'd want me to eventually run for office in Washington one day. Lexi was onboard with anything that would get us back together, and she didn't understand the words, 'we're done.' The reason we ended wasn't about cheating. She just didn't want anything out of life besides being a Harrison. I felt we grew apart in college, and she was more about shopping and getting married just to have the last name.

Antoine stepped back in the room. "Is everything all right, sir?"

"Yeah, family bullshit as usual," I said as I headed to my seat. I noticed Lexi talking with the receptionist at the front desk. "What are you doing here?" I asked when she locked her arm in mine.

Lexi sauntered inside, grinning. "I wanted to surprise you for lunch." Lexi leaned on her toes to try and kiss me.

"Lexi, we talked about this," I answered. I went to remove her grip and motioned for her to take a seat. I could tell by the amount of makeup and the tight dress she wore that she expected me to fall at her feet and cut out early to be with her. I cut off our physical relationship a year ago so as not to give her any mixed signals. I was still friendly with Lexi, just not interested in going backwards.

Lexi let out a long swoosh of air. "I know, Khalil, but I missed us," Lexi stated, crossing her legs.

"Aren't you dating some guy who works for your father?" I was happy when someone else took her mind off me.

"That didn't work out. He knew where my heart lies." Lexi dropped her purse beside her before she came around and took a seat on the edge of my desk with her legs crossed, showing off her short skirt and silky bronze-glow skin tone.

Entertaining the same fantasy of us being together is the last thing I needed today, the entire time I was with Lexi felt like a soap opera; nonstop misery of the same thing happening.

"Lexi, I have work to do, and I have lunch plans already."

A little hint of excitement shone on her face. "I know, at Savory." Lexi reached to caress my chest.

I moved her hand from me. "Who told you that?"

"I have my ways," Lexi teased and moved her right foot up against my thigh, toward my dick. I stopped her before she could move any further and stood, closing the space between us.

After dealing with Larry and now Lexi's bullshit, it was pissing me off. "Did my mother put you up to this?"

"What... No... Khalil."

I jumped up with a scowl on my face. "My father."

"No... Oh my God, can you for once stop making your parents out to be the bad guys?" Lexi argued before she pushed me away and stood.

I chuckled, wagging my finger at her. "That's your problem right there."

Lexi dropped a hand on her hip. "My problem," Lexi sassed, narrowing her brows.

Completely done with the conversation, Lexi would never change, I debated on my next words before I let them fall ignoring hurting feelings anymore.

"You're looking for validation from my parents so bad, you let it consume you." I hunched my shoulders.

Lexi stepped back in front of me. "Baby, listen..."

I gently nudged her back to give us space. "Lexi, I'm not your baby. We are done. Don't come back here again."

"You can't do that, Khalil!" Lexi sneered, cheeks heating in anger.

A throbbing headache started to creep up. Lexi would take all of this back to her parents and mine to make it a bigger situation.

"I can, and I'll let security know when I leave."

In a fuss, Lexi grabbed her purse and walked out of my office. "Security!"

I picked up the phone to tell security not to let her up anymore even if it was business related. "Tony, this is Khalil."

"Hey, Mr. Harrison," Tony replied.

"Hey... Listen, Lexi Jeffries is not allowed back up here unless it's about business."

"Are you sure, sir?" He sounded in disbelief knowing that when Lexi and I dated, she had clearance throughout the entire building without issue. Now that I was having her treated as a regular person, it was more real that we were over.

"Positive." I ended the call. Leaving for my lunch at Savory, I walked out of my office and saw Lexi talking to Antoine at the elevator. She looked to be crying. I chuckled and hit the button to step on. A text message indicated my brother was on his way to meet me. The last thing I saw was that scowl on Lexi's face as the doors closed.

5

―――――

KHALIL

I shook hands with Wasim as soon as I arrived, and he walked me over to the table my brother sat at. I'd known Wasim almost my entire life, and we'd done business together in the past. Every blue moon, I asked him for business advice.

"The legendary Khalil has made it to Savory," Wasim joked.

I rubbed my chin, slipping in the booth. "Don't act like that, Wasim. You know work keeps me busy."

"Kendall makes time to come here, and he has a business," Wasim instigated as he motioned for Eboan to bring water to our table.

Kendall laughed at his comment. "Wasim, you know Khalil stays at work twenty-four seven. He only comes out if he's not making money," Kendall jested.

I flipped them off as Eboan walked over and placed two glasses of water down, along with menus.

"Gentlemen, are you getting the usual?" Eboan remarked as he pulled out his notepad and pen.

Kendall nodded, and I started to say something when I glanced up and saw Arvon coming inside.

"Arvon. Come join us!" I called out. The restaurant wasn't too full this early, so Wasim wasn't too annoyed at me yelling across the room.

Arvon extended his hand to Kendall, Wasim, and me, then motioned for Eboan. "I can't stay. I'm picking up Nori's order and dropping Serena's keys off," Arvon followed up.

"What do you mean dropping Serena's keys off?"

"She's working today," Arvon said.

"Right now?" I investigated, scanning the restaurant to find her.

Wasim slapped a hand on my shoulder. "I see that look in your eye, Khalil. Don't hurt her," Wasim shot back before he walked back to the kitchen.

"Who is he talking about?" Kendall picked up the water to sip.

Arvon tossed his back cackling. "Serena Dunn," Arvon spoke.

Eboan perked up. "My friend Serena." Eboan fought a smile.

I shoved the menu back to him. "What do you know about her, Eboan?"

"She's sweet, smart, kindhearted, and the best mother in the world," Eboan boasted about her.

Kendall crossed his arms, looking from me to Eboan. "Is she cute?" Kendall broke into a leisurely smile.

"I'm not getting in on the conversation." Arvon ran a hand down the back of his neck.

I ignored my brother's probing and focused back on Arvon. "How much was the bill?" I asked, ready to take off any costs to take some of the burden from her.

"She needed the tires, water pump, and alternator all replaced. Came to right under five hundred." Arvon removed the receipt and handed it to me.

I pulled out my checkbook and wrote him a check for a thousand dollars. "Let's keep this between us."

"Here's your order, guys, and Arvon, your to-go bag." Eboan passed a bottle of ketchup over to Kendall and placed extra napkins down.

"Thanks," Kendall said.

"I'll see you guys later," Arvon stated, leaving Serena's keys on the table.

I picked them up and put them in my pocket. "Is Serena in the back?" I inquired.

"Do you want me to send her over?" Eboan placed the tray underneath his arm, leaving the check on the table.

"Is she in the break room?" I stood heading in that direction as Eboan followed me, chuckling at my bold stance of walking in the back of the restaurant. Wasim hated whenever I walked around the place, but he was used to me by now. I pushed the door open, looked around the kitchen, and a few staffers waved at me. I went down the hall and knocked on the break room door.

A few minutes later, a gasp was heard.

"What are you doing back here?" Serena moved away.

I could tell she was pondering on how to escape. I put the matter aside taking in her beauty and remembering why I came back here.

"I have a gift for you," I said, pulling the keys out of my pocket.

"Serena, be careful with this one," Eboan jested, walking off laughing.

Serena snatched the keys from my hands. "Eboan!

Eboan!" A shadow of alarm touched her face at being alone with me.

"I couldn't wait for dinner tonight, and I saw Arvon, so I said I'd take care of giving you your keys back."

"Thanks, but you can't be back here, Khalil." She shuffled from one foot to the other.

I slid my hands in my pockets. "Wasim doesn't mind." I closed the gap between us.

"How much do I owe you?" Serena asked, changing the subject.

I pushed her hair behind her ear. "Nothing." I licked my lips, feeling how soft it felt against my fingers.

Serena's anger lit her eyes. "You're kidding, right?"

"I took care of it."

Serena chortled. "I'm not letting you pay for my car, Khalil."

"Dinner, just the two of us," I negotiated.

"I don't date." Serena shot a cold look.

Her life and mine were very different, but something rebellious gleamed in her eyes and liked to be challenged.

I drew in her sweet scent and closed my eyes. "Good, I don't either."

"You just asked for dinner." Serena stepped back.

"You have to eat, right? I know the boys would want their mommy to eat."

"Khalil, this won't work. You and I are too different." Serena's breath came out raggedy.

I scanned around the room noticing the setup was causal and felt homely with a couch, microwave, fridge, and TV hanging on the wall.

"Then we can discuss that at dinner."

"I will think about it, but dinner tonight won't work with the kids. I have plans," Serena said.

"What type of plans?" Hearing she had other plans when we discussed potentially having the kids hang together, a part of me was curious if it involved another man.

"A girls' night out." Serena moved to clean up her stuff from the table.

I stared at her backside when she turned, the curves of her hip. "Let me guess, Dionne and Nori are making you go out for drinks at the bar," I commented.

"Yep."

I could tell she would be my blind spot.

I reached for her hand before she moved to leave. "You can bring the boys over, so they're not bored."

"I don't know. I've never left them with anyone besides my parents," Serena informed me.

"If it'll make you feel any better, you can come with them," I tested, pulling out my phone to check a text message.

> **Lexi:** *I think we should talk.*
> **Me:** *Lexi, move on.*
> **Lexi:** *I still love you.*

Serena jerked from my hold. "Girlfriend problems?" Serena avoided going out with me, but whenever she suspected a call or text she acted like my woman and questioned me.

I shoved my phone in my pants and lifted her chin. "Single, what about you?"

"Single and not looking for anything. My kids are my priority." Serena's nostrils flared with fury.

"Serena, we have an order for two dozen cupcakes." Uliana stuck her head in and informed her.

"Thanks, Uliana. I'll take care of it now." Serena put on a smile.

"I'll let you get back to work, but instead of paying me back with money, I want dinner for just the two of us," I told her before I lifted her hand and kissed the top of her palm, leaving her stuck and unable to respond. I left the employee entrance and finished lunch with my brother.

Kendall took a sip of his beer. "What took you so long?"

I lost my appetite and pushed the plate away. "I needed to give Serena back her keys. Then Lexi texted me."

"Please tell me you're not going back to her."

"No, she wants to, and I think Mom is pushing her on me," I said, still holding my phone. I noticed Lexi had sent me a photo of her in her bathing suit.

Me: *Lexi, I'm not stupid, and using my employees won't work.*

I replied and closed out of my messages.

"Stella Harrison will do anything to make the perfect family." Kendall pulled out his wallet to leave a twenty on the table.

"You knew her first," I joked as I glanced over at Serena standing at the counter talking to some guy.

"Let me guess, that's Serena... She's cute, bro," Kendall chimed in gulping down the water.

"She's gorgeous," I muttered.

Serena's head bent back in laughter.

"How do you think she'll do with Mom and Dad?" Kendall got out of the booth.

I followed suit, tossing another twenty down. "I'm not living my life by their standards anymore."

"How did the sale go today with the online company?" Kendall asked, standing at the counter.

"It closed, and he's getting below asking price."

"Hi, what can I get you?" Serena plastered on a wide smile.

She was becoming too friendly with everyone except me and I was ready to give her something to smile about.

"Hi, Serena, can I get two of the lemon cupcakes and a chocolate chip?" Kendall studied her and winked at me.

"Sure. It's the last batch of the day." Serena picked up a box and, with a pair of tongs, quickly boxed up his order.

"Serena, you know you owe me a date," the guy she was talking to stated, butting into our conversation.

I frowned, heat riding up my neck. "She's not interested," I blurted out.

Kendall, Serena, and the guy all looked at me in surprise.

"Excuse me, I think Serena can speak for herself," the guy retorted.

I started to walk toward him, and Kendall put his arm out to block me. I held my hands up to show that I wouldn't hit him.

"Khalil," Serena hissed, closing the bakery case.

I sneered at him. "Serena is already taken." I held both hands to Kendall letting him know I was cool.

"And who are you?" The man drew back in shock, ready to fight.

If he knew me, he'd keep it moving, take his cocked-eye ass somewhere else.

"Todd, let it go. Khalil, cut it out," Serena demanded as she passed Kendall the order and rang him up.

"See you tomorrow, Serena." Todd shook his head.

I tried to step around Kendall and he blocked me again. "Todd, don't let the suit fool you, friend. Serena ain't interested if you come around here again."

"Or what?" Todd chuckled, stomping toward us.

A crowd started to form and I knew Serena hated being in the spotlight.

"What's going on out here?" Wasim came from around the corner.

"Nothing. Wasim, do you need me for anything else? I need to get going for the day." Serena started to remove her apron.

"You're good to go, Serena," Wasim told her.

"Thanks," Serena said and cleaned her area. She went to the employee door.

I started to walk toward the back to find her.

Kendall caught me by the arm. "Give her some space."

He was right and I'd basically almost got her in trouble at work.

"What's up with you?" Wasim followed us.

"I'm good. I need to head out and get to work." I shook hands with him and walked out of the restaurant with Kendall next to me. My phone vibrated again in my pocket as I pulled my keys out.

"Try not to get in any fights, bro," Kendall said, patting me on the back.

My dad was calling me, I wanted to ignore it but knew he'd call back.

"Fuck you," I joked and answered the phone.

"Hello," Dad said.

"Yeah."

"Come to my office," Dad demanded.

I sighed in annoyance, opened the car door, and got inside. I stared out the window as Serena left the restaurant.

Todd matched her steps as she went to her car. I wanted to get back out and knock him on his ass. She obviously wasn't interested in him and tried to give him a hint, but he couldn't take rejection.

Focusing back on the call I started the ignition. "What do I need to come to your office about?"

"Just get here now," Dad avoided answering and ended the call.

I groaned, running my hand down my face, and drove off toward his office. I wasn't in the mood to deal with one of his campaign speeches. He had another year before re-election, and they'd started running campaigns about me in the mix, which was a lie. I had no interest in the political world.

Not long after I stopped in front of his office and headed inside ready to hear what problems I created for him. I waved at his secretary as I busted through his door, not caring if he had someone in there already. My day wouldn't be ruined with any stupid shit.

"Glad you could make it, son." Dad glanced at me over his shoulder, checking his tie in the mirror.

"What do you want?"

"I need you to come to dinner tomorrow and formally announce your engagement," Dad explained, whirling around to look at me.

"I'm not dating anyone to be asking somebody to get married."

"Lexi has talked with her father, and he called me to see what the holdup is." Dad's expression was thunderous.

"Stay out of my personal life. Lexi and I broke up a while ago."

He waved away my comment. "That doesn't matter. You buy her some flowers, take her to dinner, then get engaged." Dad grabbed a newspaper off his desk and shoved it to my chest.

"I'm not marrying somebody I don't love so you can have

some political control!" I shouted as I tossed the paper to the floor. I didn't care that he was up in the polls.

Dad stomped in my direction, got in my face. "Goddammit, Khalil, for once in your life, why can't you look at the big picture?" Dad yelled back.

I threw my hands in the air. "Because I don't want this life for myself. I'm happy where I am at," I seethed, the thought of being in a dead-end marriage spurted nightmares.

"You can still have your businesses. Why can't you do both?"

I moved back and turned to leave and he gripped my elbow. "Do you hear yourself?"

"Jeffries and Harrison could make the biggest impact in North Park and the country as a whole," Dad tempered his anger.

I snatched away, scrubbed a hand down my face. "Is that all you care about? Having power and not your child's happiness?"

"Happiness is overrated sometimes, son." Dad laughed bitterly.

"I'm not doing it."

"You're going to throw what your grandfather and I have built away?" Dad scrutinized, sitting back down in his chair.

"I can't do this with you anymore. I'm not interested."

"We already put out feelers and ran a poll with voters," Dad explained, not giving up.

"I don't care."

"Your mother wants you at dinner."

"Fine, I will come to dinner," I said, stomping out of his office, a hard grimace on my face.

I left his office and decided to head over to the bar for a few drinks, since Serena avoided a date with me and now hearing my mother wanted me to come tomorrow put me in a sour mood. I needed to drown out the noise and the back-to-back text messages from my mother and Lexi. I put fifty dollars down on the bar, and I asked for a scotch on the rocks. I unbuttoned my suit jacket and dropped my phone on top of the bar as it buzzed again.

Mom: *Don't forget dinner.*
Me: *I won't.*
Lexi: *Baby, I can't wait to see you.*
Mom: *I want you to be on your best behavior at dinner.*
Me: *Lexi, this dinner doesn't change anything.*
Mom: *Are you listening to me?*
Me: *Mom, I said I will be there, but I'm not with Lexi anymore.*
Lexi: *We can work on us, Khalil.*

She's crazy, I said to myself.

I closed the text thread and shut my phone off as I felt a pat on my back. I turned to see Arvon.

I pointed toward the bartender to get him a drink. "What's up, man?" Hanging with a friend might ease the anger from the conversation with Dad.

"I'm just passing through from the shop." Arvon thanked him.

"How are the boys?" I questioned, pouring more into my glass.

Arvon sipped on his drink. "Boys are good; they're at home with Mom."

"How is Jeanette doing?" I asked.

"Mom told me to tell you to come over for dinner when you have time," Arvon spoke.

I twirled the liquid around in the glass. "For sure do that. I love her lasagna."

"You look like shit, so what's up?"

I grunted, kicking the drink back, tapping for another one. "Family problems and Lexi."

The entire town thought we'd be the couple of year, but Lexi was too hung up on being the star and less on being genuinely in a relationship.

"Didn't you break up with her?" Arvon's mouth thinned with displeasure.

I cracked my neck. "I did, but she's close with Mom, so of course, she's wiggled her way in, thinking that could change something."

"I saw the posters of your dad's re-election campaign; they're talking about you running next."

"He can't understand that I want nothing to do with running for mayor or marrying into the Jeffries family."

Arvon's been in a long-time marriage with kids. He could see both sides from being a family man, plus wanting what's best for your children. "Be honest with him and let them know that you're your own man."

I sucked my teeth. "I hear you, but they have a one-track mind."

"Give it some time," Arvon said as his phone rang. He returned the message and smirked at me.

"What?"

"That was Nori asking if Serena could bring the boys over to hang with Jett this weekend."

I grunted, leaning over to see his reply. "So."

"I just thought you'd like to know since you paid for her car service," Arvon teased, closing his thread and finishing his drink.

I gestured, sitting up on the stool. "That was me being nice."

"You sure? Serena's a beautiful woman," Arvon

announced.

I gripped the glass tight. Something about him noticing how gorgeous she was caused a sudden protection in me, and I wanted to tell him to keep her name out of their mouths.

"Calm down, I can see that vein poking out of your forehead. I was the same way with Nori." Arvon slapped a hand on top of the bar.

"Same what?"

"You like her," Arvon suggested.

"I'm trying to not go there. My life is too complicated, and I don't want to go down a road of dating another woman who has the same mentality as Lexi."

"You don't believe that, so cut the shit out. Serena is nothing like Lexi."

I cleared my throat. "I hear you, man. But a lot of women, once they see what comes with the Harrison name? They run."

"Have you asked her out on a date?"

Arvon ignored everything I was saying making me think of earlier when I tried to get Serena to go out with me.

"Yeah, we seem to always be passing."

He leaned on the bar with his back facing the crowd. "See if there's something there and ask her out," Arvon said.

"Yeah, let me think about it."

"On that note, I need to head out. Boys want me to bring home pizza," Arvon said, slapping me on the back, and shook hands goodbye.

I turned my head, hearing the latest video from my dad on TV, talking about what he had accomplished while in office. I took the last swig of the dark liquor, left another twenty-dollar tip, and headed home for the night to get some sleep while I could. I had Serena on my mind as I tossed and turned, thinking about all the what-ifs and whether or not she would even give me a chance. I didn't know anything about the father of her boys and wondered if he was still in the picture. I wouldn't care if he were, but she seemed like the type to be loyal, and I liked that about her.

6

KHALIL

When I finished work the next afternoon, I went home to change clothes before dinner with my family. The only bright side about this dinner was seeing my niece Kayla and brother Kendall. My mom called me early this morning as I headed to work to confirm I was still coming. I said I would. She told me that Lexi would be there, yet I knew that already, so I prepared for this to be a long night full of dreadful conversation and fake smiles. Lexi thought she was slick coming to my office and trying to get me back into her claws, but I put a stop to that. I wasn't planning on drinking too much in case I needed to leave before dinner was even over. My mom liked to try out different meals to make it seem like she was worldly to any guests who came over.

Tonight, she had a French theme, and I walked into the front of their mansion and almost turned around. They had the France flag waving, music playing, and the housekeeper and butler were all dressed up. Normally, they'd be in relaxed uniforms, but they made it seem like the Queen of England was coming. I grew up here, and the place still seemed like it was too much as the mayor's home. It sat on three acres and was three stories high. I noticed more cars outside and wondered who else was here. I walked into the living room and saw my brother talking with his wife and Kayla, who was all dressed up like a little Barbie doll and looked miserable. I stepped into the room and cleared my throat. Kayla looked up and ran toward me.

"Kayla, young ladies do not run," Mom scolded, placing her drink on the table.

My brother shook his head and picked Kayla up before she started crying. "Was that necessary?" Kendall frowned with his entire weight.

Mom's lower lip shot out and came over to kiss me on the cheek. "She'll be fine. Hello, Khalil." Mom swiped along my shoulder to remove lint.

"Hey," I responded dryly, tone indicative of how much I didn't want to be here tonight.

"I want you to meet some people." Mom formed a cheeky smile.

I gently stepped back out of her hold. "I'm not in the mood."

"Get in the mood. Your father pulled a few strings to get Lexi's father and his campaign manager to come tonight," Mom stated.

"I'm not doing this." I turned to leave when Lexi came into the room holding a champagne glass.

Lexi smirked, swaying her hips. "There you are," Lexi said sweetly and tried to kiss me on the lips.

I moved out of her way, and her lips landed on the side of my chin.

Mom cupped Lexi by the arm, bumping her on the hip. "You two look so lovely together." Mom excitedly tried to grab my hand and lock it with Lexi's.

I heard giggling behind me, and Kendall's wife clasped her hand over her mouth when my mother glared at her. Bianca worked at his company in the marketing department part time while raising Kayla.

"Khalil, it's good to see you," Lexi's father said.

I groaned, crossing my hands in front of me. "Chester."

"Daddy, Khalil and I have been talking again," Lexi lied.

I opened and closed my mouth ready to say hell no when my mom cut in that dinner was ready.

"That's good, sweet pea." Chester wrapped his arms around Lexi, and they headed toward the dining room.

Kendall came next to me and popped me on the back of the head. "Dumbass," he muttered, letting Kayla down.

Bianca laughed at him. My mom held up her hand to stop her from walking any further.

"This dinner is very important to your father and me." Mom faced all of us sneering.

"So, why am I here?"

I had not missed how she made it all about them and fuck what I want for my life.

She dragged her eyes from me to Kendall. "Don't be a jackass, Khalil," Mom spat.

"Stop trying to run my life, and I won't," I argued back.

"Boy, I am your mother, and you wouldn't even be here without me. This is happening, and you need to get on board," Mom harshly spat.

A tense silence engulfed the room.

"You and Lexi need to stop trying to think I'll take her back."

The memories came crawling back; growing up and having a mother that dictated every moment of my life from the sports I wanted to play to picking my friends and dating life.

"Why not? She's perfect for you." Mom bent down to grab her drink.

"I'm interested in someone else," I blurted out, and everyone glanced at me in shock. Normally, I kept my private life just that, but they were pushing this Lexi thing, and I needed to put a stop to it immediately.

"Who is she? A part of our circle? A Chambers or maybe the Dendrite family?" Mom rattled off names.

"No." I went over to the dining room and sat across from Lexi. It looked like they had assigned seating, but I didn't care and sat as far away as possible.

Mom stood beside the empty chair. "Khalil, wouldn't it be better to sit next to your fiancée?"

I spat out my water. "What!"

"Khalil, calm down," Dad said, narrowing his eyes at me.

I glared back at him, then Lexi as she avoided eye contact with me. I lifted the napkin to clean the spill up.

"Khalil, I was under the impression you were finally thinking of running for your father's seat," Chester chimed in grabbing his fork and knife.

"If you need advice, I can help. Just give me a call," Ben, the campaign manager, put in his two cents.

I handed the plate to the staff and waited for another one. "I don't because I'm focused on my company."

"My father could help you, Khalil," Lexi commented, pinning me with a long, silent scrutiny.

"I don't need his help, Lexi."

"Khalil, stop being like this." Mom gritted her teeth.

I blew out a breath of frustration and picked up my spoon to eat whatever the hell they had in front of us. It looked like soup, but I couldn't tell.

"My son is still trying to decide what he wants to do," Dad informed everyone, taking a bite of his salad.

"Kendall signed a huge deal with a hotel chain," Bianca announced, changing the subject.

I smiled at her for trying to help.

"That's good, dear, but it's important for our family to plant Khalil in the right places." Mom ignored her and made it about them.

"I agree with your mother, Khalil. It would be good for your business to run for office and marry Lexi. Our connections could take you far," Chester explained.

It was hard to remain sane without starting another argument and walking out. "Mr. Jeffries, I'm seeing someone else," I informed him, pushing the soup away and starting on the fresh lamb.

Lexi lowered her gaze in confusion. "Who is she?" Lexi demanded.

"You don't know her." I took a sip of the wine.

"Khalil, come to talk to me in my office." Dad stood and dropped his napkin on the table before walking away.

"I have somewhere to be. Sorry, I have to go," I brought up. Winking at my brother, I jumped up and left from the dinner.

My mother yelled for me to come back inside. I didn't see anything appealing about being in a marriage with Lexi for the rest of my life, knowing she'd just sit up, shop, and complain about the amount of time we spend together. Don't get me started on having kids. One time, she tried to manipulate me into not using a condom. I soon realized she had nothing going on besides to have the name and publicity. I hopped in my car and drove over to Serena's house. I wanted to check up and see how things were going with her car and the boys.

...

I finally pulled up to her house, seeing the time on my watch. It wasn't too late. Maybe the wine made me crazy for thinking there were feelings between us. I did feel some chemistry when we first met at the car, but I tried to keep my dating life simple and uncommitted to anything serious. I knocked on the door and heard Silas and Prince calling out. The locks turned, and Silas smiled at me.

"Silas, did I tell you to wait?" Serena argued, pulling them behind her.

"It's just Khalil, Mommy," Silas muttered.

"I don't care. Go back and watch the TV." Serena turned him around and raked a hand over his head.

"Fine." Silas poked his lip out in a pout, crossed his arms, then stomped over to the couch.

Serena held the door half open. "He'll be all right. What are you doing here?"

I stepped in close, enjoying her struggle to capture her composure. "I wanted to see you," I blurted out.

Serena let the door go and met my eyes. "Have you been drinking?"

"A little, but I know what I'm saying."

I felt a lurch of excitement within her.

"Okay." Serena observed the boys and stared back in waiting silence.

I stared into her face, glancing down at the little shorts she wore that showed off her thick thighs and curves. The cropped, white T-shirt showed off her stomach.

"Khalil," Serena whispered, bringing me out of my trance.

"Fuck it," I mumbled, grasping the back of her head and capturing her lips.

She moaned into my mouth.

I groaned, feeling my dick stiffen in my pants, my hands slid down to her back. Her nearness was overwhelming.

"Ohh..." Silas and Prince said.

They caused me to realize we had an audience, and I pulled back.

She put a hand on my chest and stepped back. "Ummm..." She dropped her chin, looked back at her boys.

"I want to take you out."

Serena ran a hand up and down her thighs. "Khalil." Serena's eyelashes fluttered.

The burning sweetness of her hardened nipples drew me in and ready to take her to bed.

"I like you, Serena, and I know you're just as confused as I am."

"Khalil, I have responsibilities. What is this? Some little one-night stand for you? Why not call up an old girlfriend?" Serena snapped, pushing me outside and away from the kids, closing the door behind her.

With me coming from my parents and knowing about the process of someone making demands on your life and time I had to be sensitive on my next moves, but Serena was mine and being a mother wouldn't stop me.

"I know about your responsibilities. The boys know me, and you know we need to figure out what's between us."

Serena smacked her lips. "I'm not looking to be a hit it and quit it. I've had enough of heartbreak," Serena said.

Ready to put her mind at ease, I slowly massaged her palm.

I lifted and kissed her palm. "Please, let me take you out or better yet, we can do something here with the boys."

She looked back into the living room, then at me, biting her bottom lip. I wanted to kiss those full lips again and trail my tongue across her full breasts, down to her pussy.

"I can do dinner, but at the first sign of you acting funny, I'm out." Serena sighed, letting me pull her into my chest.

Wishing for another kiss I had to keep my thoughts to myself. I pulled her close to me and we stared into each other's eyes. Goosebumps filled her arms.

"I promise I'll be on my best behavior. But I won't apologize for how I feel." I kissed the top of her forehead then her cheek, and walked back to my car, leaving her stuck in wonder about what would come of our night together.

...

The next night, I had a car service pick up Serena and bring her to my place. Edith cooked roast peppers, pasta, baked potatoes, and lobster. Dressed down in a pair of jeans and a dark-grey sweater, I chilled the wine and had cupcakes from Savory as dessert. When I heard the front bell ring, I started toward the door and checked myself in the mirror to try to calm my nerves. I'd had my share of women, but something about this woman made me want to give her everything she wanted and needed. I opened the door, and Serena smiled up at me. My mouth was wide open in shock at what she wore.

"What are you wearing?" I asked.

"What's wrong with it?" Serena looked down at her black cocktail dress that fitted every curve on her body.

I leaned against the door and closed my eyes, counting down in my head to keep me from lusting after her all night. "You're not playing fair."

Serena giggled and stepped inside.

I closed the door and licked my lips, staring at her ass. "Damn," I mumbled under my breath. "I don't see how you have two boys."

Serena trembled in my arms. "Don't let the dress fool you. The number of hours in labor and stretch marks remind me of having two boys," Serena joked.

I turned her around to get a full look and gave her a quick tour.

Serena gestured to the paintings on the wall of van Gogh. "You have a beautiful home." Serena paused in the hallway.

"Are you comfortable with dinner here? I know I said it was a surprise."

"It's fine. I already checked with Arvon and Nori to see if you were cool." Serena giggled, tugging on my hand.

I laughed at her statement. "You basically investigated me."

"Yep. I have two boys. I can't take a chance," Serena reminded me.

I took her down the hall to the dining room.

Edith was coming out of the kitchen with her purse and jacket, getting ready to leave. "Khalil, you're set for dinner," Edith expressed.

"Thanks, Edith. This is Serena."

Edith's been with me for years making sure I have three meals a day, groceries when she's not here, and I can keep up on my regimen.

"Hi." Edith reached out.

Serena grasped her hand for a shake. "Nice to meet you, Edith," Serena stated.

"You too. Have a good night, and I'll see you tomorrow," Edith replied, walking out.

I showed Serena the rest of my home. I loved hanging different African artifacts and statues or buying from local artists.

"You have a beautiful home," Serena said again.

"Thanks. I know it's kind of a bachelor pad, but it's just me." I motioned for her to follow me into the kitchen. I bought my house about five years ago and expanded when I realized I wanted a forever home. I'd had Lexi here a few times, but she'd never lived here. I liked my privacy, and marriage wasn't on my mind. I could fly out to England or Greece in a second for business and be gone for months. So, the idea of having a wife at home who needed to depend on me to keep her happy and entertained wasn't on my agenda.

I picked up the bottle of white wine and filled the glasses. "Would you like something to drink?"

The oven warmed the spacious kitchen and the spicy aroma of chicken filled the space.

"Sure... Who all lives here?" Serena asked.

I placed the top back on and handed it to her and moved beside her. "Me."

"Edith's your cook?" Serena took a sip, scanning the room.

They way the lighting bounced against her smooth silky skin pushed more thoughts down to my dick.

"Yeah, and sometimes she stays here if it's too late. Overall, I stay here by myself."

Serena squinted at me. "What do you want from me, Khalil?"

I captured her wrist and stepped in close. "Everything."

She choked on her drink.

I patted her back to help her, cleaning the spill with paper towels.

The low rumble of jazz playing in the background reminded me this was our first date and to slow down.

A flood of goosebumps scattered on her arms. "What if I can't give you everything?"

"I can't explain what this is between us, but from the

second I saw you on the freeway, I've never stopped thinking about you," I said.

She sighed, taking a step back to put space. "I'm still recovering from my ex-boyfriend cheating and leaving me. Honestly, I'm afraid of falling for someone else."

"What happened?" I took her by the hand walking us to the living room taking a seat on the couch.

"I moved down here about seven months ago after living with my parents once I finally had the courage to leave him. Jaylen is selfish," Serena grumbled, crossing her legs.

I stitched an arm on the back of the couch. "Is he in their lives?" I investigated, breath solidified in my chest.

"Hell no. Jaylen is too hung up on living life and being up with some other woman to take the responsibilities as a father seriously."

"Do you still love him?" I questioned.

Depending on the conversation it would let me know the best way to approach moving forward, especially if he ever wants to come back to his boys' lives.

Her stomach grumbled. "I thought I did when I was staying with my parents, but I realized the love I had for him was gone." She blushed, looking away in embarrassment.

I stood to get our food from the kitchen, grabbed the plates that were already set from the oven she'd covered and she followed me toward the dining room with our glasses.

"You're too beautiful to be broken up over an idiot who doesn't realize what he has in you," I told her while I placed her plate down and pulled her chair out.

Serena snickered behind closed lips. "Thanks. It took awhile, and Dionne told me the same thing, to get to a space where I wasn't stuck on him anymore," Serena remarked.

"What about your parents?"

"My parents were a big help, but they're very judgmental

and demanding. They actually want me to get back with him." Serena's face fell in disappointment, then she took a bite of her food.

I looked up, now fully in her eyes. "You're kidding, right?"

To see how much we had in common with both sets of parents trying to run our lives gave me even more clarity. A person who has complete power over others becomes even more wicked in dictating things.

Serena pushed her food around the plate. "Nope, my mom called me a few weeks ago about Jaylen wanting to see me."

I raised glass for another sip. "What did you say to her?"

"I told her no and that I was moving on with my life," she answered, a host of emotions crisscrossed her face.

"Kind of have the same situation with my parents. They have my life planned for me, and I continue to break the rules and focus on what I want. That puts a strain on us."

She fluttered her lashes. "What do they want you to do?"

"Run for mayor."

Serena drew in a breath. "Oh," she said, pushing some hair out of her face.

"My father's the current mayor, and my grandfather was previously."

The impulse to reach out and touch her was almost a tangible urge. I was ready to move into a new subject of the evening because she caused dreams I never wanted to pop in my head for the future with having a wife, even more kids.

"You don't want to carry on the legacy?"

"It comes with certain restrictions I'm not willing to give in to," I said before I reached over and captured her hand, gently squeezing.

"What do you mean?" she questioned.

"Let's not talk about my crazy family. Tell me about yourself."

The sparkle in her eyes was hesitant. Maybe I was moving too fast with her, but something told me that what I felt was being well-received, judging by the lingering stares whenever we were in each other's presence.

She hunched her shoulders. "Khalil, you know I am a single mother of twin boys, I work at Savory, and love to bake."

The magnetic pull her smile brought me sent shock waves to my heart.

"Silas and Prince, right?"

"Yep, they keep me on my toes." She laughed and tossed a piece of broccoli in her mouth.

Ready to explore the rest of the evening I angled our plates to the side.

"I have cupcakes if you want to try them," I said, standing up to walk in the kitchen.

She put her fork down with her lip poked out. "Where did you get them?" she questioned.

I snapped my fingers coming back toward her. "As a matter of fact, Savory."

She burst into laughter, and I didn't know what was so funny until she pointed at the cupcakes in my hand.

I paused, felt a ringing impulse that I'd brought in something familiar. "These are your cupcakes?" I put them on the table and removed the wrapper that Edith had covering them. I wasn't too much into sweets but for her, I'd try anything.

She nodded in answer, picking up her napkin and smaller plate. "I can't believe they sold you my cupcakes," Serena teased.

"You work as a waitress, and you do the baking? My mom is always going on about the cupcakes at Savory."

"Tell her thank you. It's one of my passions, and I'm saving up to open my own shop one day," she said, reaching out to grab the watermelon tart cupcake.

One thing about me; when it came to business I was a beast in helping to execute plans and if she needed anything from money to a building I could make it happen.

"What's your timeframe for opening it?"

Her chin pulled in, licking the icing off her finger.

I almost jumped across the table to kiss the remnants of icing on her upper lip, but remembered it was our first date.

"My goal is two to three months. I'm saving now and looking at properties," Serena told me.

I winked at her, leaving the other half of the cupcake on the plate, while I took in her calm energy. "I can't wait to be the first person in line."

We continued talking when time got away from us, and I saw it was around midnight. I had us in front of the fireplace in my backyard, talking about our lives. It started to get chilly, so I brought a blanket out to cover her up, and she dozed off. I tapped her on her shoulder.

"You ready to head home?" I probed, tracing a hand down her cheek.

She muttered something incoherent and her light snores picked up.

Deciding to call it a night, I picked her up and carried her to the guest bedroom down the hall from my room. I laid her on top of the covers, kissed her forehead, and closed the door.

7

―――――――

SERENA

I opened my eyes, feeling around the bed, then my body checked why I was in my outside clothes, and noticed I wasn't in my bedroom. Slowly I crawled back against the headboard and scanned the room, trying to remember where I was. I glanced over at the clock on the night table and saw it was going on nine a.m. Normally, I was up around seven to get breakfast going for the boys. I jumped out of bed, grabbed my purse and heels, and walked downstairs, smelling bacon and eggs. Finally stepping in the kitchen I saw Khalil drinking coffee as Edith turned over some eggs.

"Morning," Khalil greeted.

I smiled, feeling overdressed and out of place. "Hey. I didn't realize I overslept."

"I have some bacon and eggs if you're hungry. Plus, coffee or tea," Edith announced, holding up a plate of fruit.

I gazed down at my clothes ready to get out of there. All night I had to keep my heart from bursting at how sweet and kind Khalil was being with me. A man like him could have any woman he wanted, but he wanted to spend time with me.

"I'm fine, thank you."

"Take a seat. I won't bite," Khalil instructed.

I scratched the side of my head.

Edith grinned and turned the stove off, stepping out of the kitchen.

"I have to get to my boys and head to work," I reminded him of my responsibilities.

"No worries. Dionne texted and said she would get them off to school," Khalil said, reaching over to pull the chair out next to him.

I sawed out a bitter laugh at my best friend jumping the gun. "Do you have an extra toothbrush? I really need to get to work though."

"In the guest bathroom... I already spoke with Wasim, and you can come in late if you want or take the day off." Khalil's mouth pressed into a straight line.

I swung my head in a no. "I could use the time to work on my business."

"Or take my card and have a spa day for yourself and shop on me. You're always doing for everyone else," Khalil commented.

"I appreciate the offer, but I can't take your money."

"Look, Serena, I'm not trying to buy you. I genuinely like you and want to see you again. Take the morning to get your hair and nails done. Then we can go to lunch together," Khalil remarked, as he picked up his cup of coffee and took a sip.

I was stuck on if I should take him up on his offer or go to work when my phone vibrated. I picked it up and saw a text message from Dionne.

Dionne: Checking to see if you're alive.
Me: Yes, I'm fine.
Dionne: He said you overslept.
Me: I did and now I'm trying to figure out if I should stay.
Dionne: The boys are fine. Take a day for yourself.
Me: Would that be selfish?
Dionne: No, Serena. The man is offering to show you a good time.
Me: Yeah, with his money.
Dionne: Why is that a bad thing?
Me: I won't be bought, Dionne.
Dionne: There's a difference between being bought and getting spoiled.

"What's your answer?" Khalil stated, putting his plate in the sink with his coffee cup.

Dionne: Hello?
Me: Call you later.

"Fine, I can spend the day playing hooky." I closed my phone and walked back upstairs toward the bathroom to brush my teeth and wash my face.

He smiled.

Twenty minutes later, I came back downstairs, and Khalil was standing at the door with his jacket and keys.

"First, I'll drop you at home so you can get changed. I need to run by the office for a few hours," Khalil said.

"Sounds great. I haven't had a day for myself in a while."

"I know. Dionne said you're doing for the boys all the time or for someone else," Khalil reminded me and shook his head in disappointment.

"I tend to take on everyone's problems and need to spend more time on myself."

He held the door for me to hop in and jogged around to jump in putting his phone down.

Khalil eased from his driveway and slowed down at the stop sign. Leaning over, he grabbed the back of my head, entwined our lips, and slipped his tongue inside.

I moaned and gripped his tie, bringing him in closer as a car horn behind us went off.

"Let me get you home before we cross that line," Khalil said, and his Bluetooth went off in his car.

"Are you going to get that?" I checked.

He continued to let the phone ring for the fourth time. "It's nobody important." Khalil turned at the green light and arrived in front of my driveway. He went to get out.

I stopped him. "Thanks for last night. I had a good time."

"I did too, but it's not over yet. I want to see you for lunch. Come by my office around one," Khalil said, then pecked me on the lips.

He lifted his head, pinning me with a feral look.

"Okay, text me the address." I quickly kissed him again, jumped out of his car, and ran toward my door. I knew he'd fuss at me for opening the door and not waiting on him. I unlocked my front door, stepped inside, and shut it behind me. Leaning against the door, I closed my eyes and tried to calm my beating heart. *Could I really date him?* I shook my head and dropped my purse on top of the couch. When my phone buzzed, I picked it up, seeing Khalil's name.

> *Khalil: You think you're slick.*
> *Me: What are you talking about?*
> *Khalil: Mhmmm...*
> *Me: See you at lunch.*

I put my phone back down and headed to my bedroom

to undress. I needed to make sure I did inventory of replenishing cupcakes at Savory and set up appointments with realtors for my shop. It felt like I had a new burst of energy to accomplish my goals after talking with Khalil. I turned the shower on, pinned my hair up, and stepped under the hot water. I ran a washcloth with pineapple bodywash over my arms and stomach, thinking about my night with Khalil. He was a perfect gentleman, not rushing anything between us. I smiled and ran the water over the soap.

After my shower, I rubbed lotion over my body and threw on a fresh pair of loose, wide-angle pants and a half-crop top. I knew Khalil said to go to a spa or something, but I wanted to take advantage of shopping and grabbing a few things for the boys. I wasn't planning to use his money anyway. I loved to see their little faces when they came home and saw a new toy or outfit. I slid into my wedge heels, combed my hair out, and pulled it back into a high bun. With a little clear lip gloss on and some mascara, I felt refreshed and clean like a brand new me. Usually, I didn't like showing off too much of my body after having my boys but based on Khalil's eyes from last night, there was nothing wrong with the extra curves. Jaylen never showed any interest in my body after the boys came while we were together.

In my car, I turned up the radio to Rihanna blasting and put the window down. Before heading to the mall, I stopped at the gas station and parked in the first open spot. When I got out to pay, someone called my name.

"Serena!" I heard again and looked behind me, and my eyes spread wide. It was the last person I expected to see. Based on the last time we spoke, he was in Nashville with his girlfriend and their kids.

"Jaylen, what are you doing here?" I stood next to my door with my phone in my hands.

Jaylen scrunched up his face. "I came down here to talk with you after I spoke with your parents," Jaylen mentioned.

I side-eyed him. "Why are you talking to my parents?" I grilled, crossing my hands over my chest.

"Because I want to see my kids, and you changed your number," Jaylen grunted.

I waved a hand in his face. "So, after all this time, you want to see your kids. Please run that line with someone else."

"You're out here half-dressed and got my kids not knowing anything about their brothers and sisters," Jaylen spat.

I shot him a dirty look, poking him in the chest. "How dare you get in my face after you cheated on me constantly!"

Jaylen slid his hands in his pockets. "I work hard, and I may have made a few mistakes, but that doesn't mean I didn't love you," he retorted, scanning his eyes up and down my body licking his lips.

Every lie continued to spill and boil my blood, Jaylen thought I was the same old Serena blind to his chaos.

"You expect me to be dumb enough to listen to this crap."

"I expect my woman to do as she's told, pack her shit up, and get back to Nashville." His voice darkened in tone.

"Well, good thing I'm not your woman." I turned with my back to him heading to the store.

He gripped my arm and pushed me up against the car. "Shut the fuck up and get my kids!" Jaylen shouted.

I muttered low, not wanting to cause a commotion. "Take your hands off me. Our kids are in school and doing good out here. I don't know what my parents told you."

"They said you've gone crazy and ran off leaving them alone," Jaylen told me.

I chuckled at his response and jerked out of his hold. "I'm perfectly sane."

Jaylen's veins bulged over his temple. "Are you going to get them, or do we need to get the courts involved?" Jaylen tested.

"Please get the courts involved; I'm still waiting on child support." I jumped back in my car, not caring if I ran him over. I pulled out fast as he hopped back and cursed me out. I drove another two blocks to the next station and filled up my car and soon after ended up at the mall, glancing around at the sale they had running in Neiman Marcus. I stared over the dresses and continued picking through the ball-gowns and cocktail dresses. I heard giggling behind me. I looked back to see the same older woman and young girl from Savory the other day. I rolled my eyes and went on checking out dresses as they loudly talked.

"This would be perfect, Lexi," Stella spoke.

"You think, Mama Stella? Khalil won't think it's too revealing?" Lexi quizzed.

That caused my ears to perk up at his name.

"I know my son, Lexi. This would be cute, and we can have him escort you to dinner at the award ceremony," Stella said.

"Okay, I will try it on. But are you sure Khalil is going to come around?" Lexi inquired.

I inched a little closer, but they didn't pay me any attention.

"That boy of mine drives me crazy, but he loves you." Stella passed her another dress to try on.

I heard enough for the day and decided to leave without purchasing anything, debating if I should go up to his job for lunch or not, but maybe it was a good thing. I could let him know that I wasn't trying to get involved in any love triangle. I had two boys to think about; being involved in some mess wouldn't work for me. I already had Jaylen down my throat talking crazy.

I got in my car and decided to go up to Khalil's job and let him know this was the end of the road for us before I got my heart broken.

...

I parked in the visitor section and looked up at his massive office building. It had to be about forty floors tall and covered an entire block in the business district. I walked through security and went to the receptionist's desk. I never texted him that I was coming, so hopefully, I was allowed to go up without any problems.

"Hello. How can I help you?" the receptionist asked.

I swung my purse on my shoulder, fiddling with my fingers. "Hi, I'm here to see Khalil."

She typed on her computer.

"Is he expecting you? What's your name?" she asked.

"He is, but it was around one p.m. I'm early. Serena Dunn."

She continued on her computer, printed out a label with my name on top, and passed it to me. "Take this and go up to floor twenty-seven," she instructed.

I walked to the elevator and punched the button for his floor. The elevator stopped, the doors opened, and I stepped on floor twenty-seven to a gang of people talking and laughing at the front desk. I assumed it was Khalil's attractive male assistant. I cleared my throat, and the women moved out of my way.

He grinned, extending his hand. "Hey, Serena, right?"

"Yeah, and you're... Antoine." I looked down at his name plate and reached out to shake his hand.

He gestured to Khalil's closed door. "I am. I know it's weird seeing a guy as an assistant. Khalil's been like a mentor to me forever. You can go ahead on inside. He finished his meeting early," Antoine said.

"Thanks," I replied, then walked over to his office door. I lightly knocked and pushed the oak wood door open.

He waved me to come in as he continued on the phone.

I ambled around the room and checked the layout that complemented his personality. The couch and chairs were all sleek with silver and black trim. A bar sat in the corner while large paintings hung on the wall.

"Sorry about that, babe." Khalil hung up his phone and motioned for me to come to him.

"No worries; you're a busy man," I said and kept distance between us. He didn't like that, so he came around his desk, wrapped his hands around my waist, and kissed the top of my forehead.

He eased on the edge of his desk with me in between his legs. "What makes you hesitant to smile at me?" Khalil probed.

I cleared my throat and tried to step back, his grip tightened. "I saw your girlfriend and mom at the mall."

"I don't have a girlfriend," Khalil replied, running his hand up my arm, toward my shoulder, and lifted my chin.

"Lexi." All of my senses wanted to reach out and say they're perfect for each other because it would never work if we dated.

"My ex-girlfriend," Khalil said, eyes glinting with pure masculine interest.

"Khalil, what are we doing exactly?"

He tucked his bottom lip between his teeth. "Hopefully we're getting to know each other and growing into like," Khalil joked.

Little could put me in a bad mood beside Jaylen, or my parents, so coming to terms with everything felt right to admit and be honest. The city outside roared and felt like it matched the pounding of my heartbeat. "I saw my ex today."

His body tensed up at the mention of Jaylen. "Where?" He backed up and slid his hands in his pockets.

"I was on my way to the mall and stopped for gas."

We stood in front of his window, looking out at the traffic and passersby hailing cabs.

Khalil jerked his head, his face screwed up. "What does he want?" Khalil questioned.

"For me and the boys to pack and go back to Nashville."

Khalil grasped my hand, pulling it up to his lips. "What do you want?" Khalil asked.

"I'm doing what I want, and that's raising my kids and building my business."

"Any room for me in those plans?" Khalil commented as he raised my palm up and entwined our hands.

"Honestly, I don't know, Khalil. I like you, that's not the problem. But your world and mine are different."

"A different world doesn't mean we need to stop what could be a great future for us both," Khalil stated, closing the space.

I put my hands on his chest. "I told Jaylen, and I'm telling you the same thing. I'm not playing the role as a side girlfriend to you."

"I wouldn't expect you to." Khalil leaned down and skimmed his lips along the sweep of my cheek.

I sank into his body instantly, the hard planes of his muscles holding me.

He pulled back and stared into my eyes. "Let's go to lunch," Khalil suggested and turned to grab his keys and wallet off his desk.

I followed next to him as we walked out of his office.

He told his assistant he was leaving for lunch. "Where do you want to go?" Khalil asked.

"Let's go to Jones," I said. Not wanting to get bombarded at work, I opted for an alternate place.

"I will ride with you," Khalil said as we stepped on the elevator.

"What about your car?" I questioned.

As the doors closed, he pushed me back to the corner, dropped his hands on both sides of me, and bit my bottom lip. He reached out and bracketed my waist, rubbing the arc of my hip bone with his thumbs.

"I can't get enough of your lips, baby," Khalil moaned, as we played tongue hockey.

8

————

KHALIL

I opened the door to Jones and let Serena walk inside first. The hostess took us to the back booth to have a seat. It wasn't too crowded around this time, so we'd be able to talk and figure out what we were going to do. I refused to let her slip out of my hands.

"Here you go. Your waitress will be out in a second," the hostess informed us, passing a menu to each of us.

Serena removed her jacket, laying it on the seat. "Thank you." Serena flipped the menu open.

"So, tell me about your plans for the business," I said, wanting to see what I could possibly do to help her business.

She smiled, clasping her hands together on top of the table. "I have a name and concept of what I want to sell."

"How big of a shop are you thinking?" Listening to every word, I made a note to myself to get my assistant every piece of information to scout locations.

Our waitress stepped in and interrupted placing glasses down and filling them with water before taking our order for drinks.

"Hello. I'm Sally, and I'll be your waitress."

"Hello, can I get a lemonade and bacon grilled sandwich?" Serena called off.

"Sure. Anything for you, sir?" Sally asked, taking down Serena's order on her notepad before she picked up her menu.

"I'll get the burger and fries with a lemonade as well."

"Perfect. I'll be right back with your drinks and get your orders in," Sally said as she headed back to the kitchen.

Getting back to conversation she continued about her dreams.

"Nothing too big, but I'd like to hire two to three people," Serena mentioned.

"Would you quit working at Savory?" I inquired.

"Yeah, that's one of the things that will have to go, but Wasim is understanding."

For as long as I've known Wasim and most of the small town business owners here, everyone supported each other and would help out if needed. For my family alone we've been long time customers of his so I'd expect he'd support her in any shape or form.

"Have you looked at locations?"

"I looked at a few places on Main Street, and I need to set up appointments," Serena said, grabbing her napkin to put on her lap.

"I know a few realtors who can help you."

Serena sipped on her drink. "You don't have to do that, Khalil."

"I know I don't. Let me do this for you as a friend."

"So, we're friends," she answered, arching her brow.

"Friends who are growing into something more."

"I think you'd be too much for me," she stated, voice running together in a velvet sound.

"How so?" My mind thumbed through all the women I have dealt with that probably would agree with her statement, especially knowing my family's habit of butting in and trying to run my life.

"You seem like the intense type who would put your entire life into making some woman happy."

I stretched a palm across the table, gripping her hand. "If she was worth it, yes, but I haven't found anyone who makes me want to give my all."

She shifted in her seat and peered around the restaurant, so as not to keep eye contact.

"Until you."

Serena reeled back and stared at me. "What are you saying?" she asked.

I pointed between us. "I am saying don't let anything my family says, or even my ex, get in the middle of this. I can't promise marriage and kids. I was never the type to lie."

She hunched her shoulders, sat forward. "I'm not looking for a husband."

"Then we're clear on what we want." Sally returned, placing our food down on the table, and set down extra napkins.

I released her hand and took a bite of my food. "What's your budget for the shop?"

"Last time I calculated, it would be around fifty thousand," she recalled, pouring sauce on her burger.

"My brother has his own construction company. He'd give you a great deal," I announced chewing on my food, before I picked up my phone and texted Kendall to contact her.

Me: *Yo, bro. I need a favor.*
Kendall: *What's up?*

> *Me: Serena is looking into opening a business.*
> *Kendall: Your girlfriend from Savory?*

I wasn't ready to give too much information on what we are yet to anybody, keeping it a secret gave us time and space to enjoy ourselves.

> *Me: Just meet with her.*
> *Kendall: Sure, tell her to call me.*
> *Me: Thanks.*

Serena licked her lips, removing some of the ketchup. "What are you smiling at?"

I took a napkin and cleaned the rest away grinning. "My brother Kendall wants you to call him to go over your plans for the shop."

"Really! How much is he charging?" Serena asked as she wrapped her lips around the straw and took a sip of her lemonade.

I covered my mouth as I chewed and rubbed my hands together. I needed to control myself; my dick was now pushing against my zipper, wanting to meet her lips.

I started to answer when we were interrupted by the same brown eyes I grew up with that could steal the joy out of a room if you didn't agree with her.

"Khalil, who's this?" Mom asked, while Lexi glared at Serena.

"This is Serena, my girlfriend," I lied. Lexi gasped in shock.

Serena choked on her drink, and my mom almost fainted. I jumped up to help her sit and passed her a glass of water.

"Khalil, what the hell are you doing?" Lexi fussed as she stepped in my face.

I stepped around her. "Lexi, get out of my face."

"No, who is she... Wait! I've seen her before," Lexi stated, snapping her fingers.

"Khalil, why are you driving me into an early grave? Your father and I won't put up with this," Mom demanded before she grabbed the glass out of my hand to finish off the water.

I sat back in the booth. "Put up with what?" I ripped out the words impatiently.

Mom pointed between me and Serena. "Dating the help!" she shouted.

Serena's eyes darted between my mom and me, then she grabbed her things to leave.

I blocked her exit and forced her to sit back down.

"I knew I remembered her from Savory." Lexi folded her arms.

Serena tried to keep her composure, tension sipped from her voice. "Khalil, I need to leave, and you can talk with your family," Serena finally spoke.

I swallowed a knot in my throat, shook my head no. "You don't have to leave."

Lexi reached to shove me back from Serena. "Yes, she does!" Lexi shouted.

"Lexi's right. This girl works as a waitress, and you think she's going to represent my family at the award event," Mom rambled on.

I sighed and ran a hand on the back of my head to tamp down my temper. "Serena, grab your things. We're leaving." I reached for her hand.

She was hesitant at first, but my eyes pleaded with hers to leave with me. She finally took my hand, and we walked out with my mom and Lexi yelling behind us.

"What do you think your father is going to say about this?" Mom yelled and tried to block us.

I held a stern facial expression. "There's nothing wrong with what Serena does, but if you must know, she's starting her own business. She makes desserts at Savory."

"Wait, you're the cupcake girl," Mom whispered.

"That's me," Serena muttered. She released my hand and got in the passenger seat of her car.

"Khalil, my father will hear about this." Lexi scowled and stomped toward my mother's car.

Mom's mouth took on an unpleasant twist. "Khalil, you need to rethink whatever it is you're doing and focus on Lexi and the future you both will have when you're running for mayor," Mom said.

"That's what you don't get, Mother dear. I'm not running for mayor. I don't know how many times I have to tell you," I said as I kissed the side of her cheek, got in the driver's side, and reversed out of the parking spot. In the rearview mirror, I could see Mom shouting in her phone. I gazed over at Serena, and she was texting back and forth with someone.

"Sorry about our lunch date."

Her eyes were filled with curious longing. "I know," she spoke.

"I need to get back to the office and finish working. Can I come over afterwards?" I checked, turning at the light.

"Not tonight. I need to spend some time with my kids and get some things together for my meeting," she said.

I captured her eyes. "Who are you texting?" I inquired.

"Dionne," she sighed, hand on the door.

I pulled up to my office building. I put the car in park and looked over at Serena. "Look at me," I said.

Her eyes moved upward from chest to face. "What?" she asked.

"My family doesn't speak for me or decide my choices. Lexi will find the next rich guy and forget about me soon."

"Okay," she answered.

"Do you believe it?" I was relieved we were alone but felt the wall coming back up of wanting to avoid me again.

"It's not a matter of me believing you. Do you believe you're ready to take on a relationship and two boys? It's a package deal, my friend," Serena replied as she dropped her phone in her lap, then folded her hands together.

"I will let my actions speak for themselves." I cupped her chin, meshing our lips together as she tried to pull back. I pushed the seat back and pulled her into my lap for a make out session. My hands roamed up her back as she moaned until a knock came at her window.

"Sorry... Mr. Harrison, we have a line of cars behind you," Christian, the valet, said barging in on our moment.

I groaned and nodded.

Serena quickly moved back over to her seat in embarrassment.

I laughed at her and pulled over to the side where the cars got ready to leave.

Serena jumped out fast so she could get to the driver's side.

"I apologize about what happened today. But it doesn't change what I want."

"You might want me, Khalil, but will they allow it is the question," Serena spoke the words and drove from the parking space, not letting me answer.

Deep down, I felt I could control my mom and Lexi, but my father was something unpredictable. I stepped back into the building and finished up some phone calls and reports on a new prospective business I was interested in buying when my office door opened with Antoine peeking in, looking uneasy.

"What's up?"

"Your father is here," Antoine mumbled.

I rubbed a hand over my forehead. "Shit! Hold my calls for now."

Antoine opened the door wider, and my father glared at him. I motioned for him to leave and that I'd be okay. My dad sat in front of my desk, nostrils flared, and I guessed my mom would have had him here sooner and not an hour later.

I dropped the messages on the desk and slumped down in my chair. "I take it Mom called you."

"What are you doing flaunting around town with some waitress!" Dad yelled.

I sat up in my seat, glaring at him. "First off, lower your voice. This is *my* place of business." I pointed at myself.

He raised up with both elbows on my desk. "A business you were provided with off my name, boy," Dad said.

I dipped my head, counting to three before staring back at him. "That's probably why you always think someone owes you something."

"I think you need to figure out what you're going to tell that little girlfriend of yours."

"Her name is Serena, and I'm not leaving her, so you and Mom can get used to her being around," I demanded. Standing I slammed my hand on top of the desk.

"That girl has nothing that she could bring to our legacy, and you want to play some stepdaddy to her kids!" Dad's face twitched.

I stopped, inhaling a deep breath. "She's working at the Savory part time and working on her business."

"You found her on the side of the road, boy," Dad spat, expression clouded in anger.

"I'm doing my best to try to respect you as my father, but if you continue down this path, I'll forget who you are and kick your ass," I yelled, standing out of my seat.

"First, your brother and now you. Where did we go wrong?" Dad paced around the room.

"This fake perfect family isn't what I want for myself with Lexi. I told you and Mom that plenty of times."

Dad took a seat on the couch. "Son, you have a chance to go far with your career. Why stick to just running a business?"

"I'm not doing this with you anymore. If you want to be in my life, I suggest you and Mom accept who I'm with as well as her kids. Are we getting married? No. But she means a lot to me," I explained as I came around my desk and stood in front of him.

"I think you're making a mistake. I heard the father of her children is here in town," Dad reminded me, a shadow of alarm touched his face.

"She already told me."

"She has too much baggage, Khalil. I hope you know what you're doing." Dad grimaced, then clapped a hand on my shoulder.

"I'll be fine."

"How is the dealership coming along?" Dad questioned.

I had recently invested in owning a car dealership that Wasim informed me about, and I wanted to branch out into more markets once we got more foreign cars on the lot. "Things are good. Wasim gave me great advice," I said, and my father nodded and started to walk out.

"Lexi called her father, and he phoned me on my way

over here. We have the award dinner next month. I expect you there."

I promised I would come a few months back. It was an annual award ceremony for the local community and helped honor those who did extraordinary things. My father was receiving an award for his work in building community centers in the low-income neighborhoods. He really only did things that benefited him, and building those centers gave them an incentive to put their own businesses in the spot to make money. I didn't agree with what they did, so I stayed out of the political side of things. Kendall also turned them down; he'd basically be selling his soul to the devil. I watched my dad leave, and I went back to my desk to finish working and try to get over the longest week ever. I needed to prepare myself for the award ceremony and convince Serena to go with me and be in the same room as my mom and Lexi.

9

———

SERENA

*O*ne month later.

Things with Khalil took off fast after the hiccup at Jones, but on the bright side, my boys adored him. We went on some dates together, like old-school drive-in movies and dinner. He helped me map out a plan for my business and introduced me to a few realtor friends. I finally had time to go out and see some buildings, and Kendall was a big help with knowing what to look out for in the space I wanted. Today, Khalil asked me to come up to his car dealership. I had no clue why I needed to meet him there since I had an appointment to get my hair done in two hours, before the award dinner. At first, I was hesitant to be in a room with his ex and his parents. They seemed like I was beneath the Harrison family and thought Khalil should only be with Lexi to further their agenda. I picked up the bottle of water and waited for Khalil to come back into the lobby. I checked out some of the cars from the most expensive BMWs to Lexus and Range Rovers.

"Which one?" Khalil headed down, signed some papers for an employee, and thanked them.

"What?" I asked.

"Which car do you like?" Khalil slid his hands in his pockets.

I gestured at the corner area. "They all look good. In a dream world, I'd take a Jeep or SUV type of car with the kids."

"Tommy, grab the keys to the four-door Rover," Khalil said to the guy who took the papers out of his hands.

I stood there, blank, amazed and very shaken. "Khalil."

"You need a new car, and I'm not taking no for an answer," Khalil commented.

I lowered my gaze in confusion. "I don't need a new car."

"That car of yours won't last much longer, and the boys are getting bigger. You're taking the car," Khalil announced and took the keys out of Tommy's hand.

"Khalil, I can't afford a new car with me saving for my shop."

"I did not ask you to pay for it, baby. I'm giving you the car." Khalil pressed a kiss on my lips.

I fell into his chest, groaning. "I'm not with you for your money."

He rubbed up and down my back, kissed the top of my head. "I own the dealership. You're my girlfriend, and I know you took the car to Arvon again because the engine was acting weird."

I rolled my eyes. I told Arvon not to say anything to him.

He pushed the keys in my hand, then grinned.

I pouted, feeling so conflicted. "Arvon wasn't supposed to tell you that."

"Don't be mad. But I want you to have this car," Khalil said.

"Fine, but no more gifts." My mind was spinning with bewilderment.

"I can't promise that," Khalil said while he stretched his arm around my shoulder and walked me over to the car.

I opened the door, slid inside, and ran my hands over the steering wheel.

"You look good behind the wheel, baby," Khalil teased, pressing a kiss on my lips.

"Thank you." I jumped back out of the car and extended my arms around his neck.

He bent down to kiss me.

"What time are you picking me up tonight?" I asked.

"Around seven. They usually last about three hours, but I usually don't last long," Khalil stated. He walked me up against the door, burying his head between my neck and shoulder. We hadn't taken it to the next level and had sex yet. Our schedules kept us busy, but I was nervous if we did take that leap, would all of this end after he got what he wanted in the end?

I had to constantly tell myself Khalil wasn't like Jaylen.

"Thanks for the car, but I need to head out to get my hair done."

He ran a hand over my hair. "Okay. Call me when you make it home," Khalil said as he kissed me on the lips.

I turned to look back at the car. "What about my old car?"

"I'll take care of the car," Khalil remarked.

Khalil passed me the paperwork, and I filled out all of my information.

Once we finished and talked with the dealer, I pulled out of the lot and drove away feeling amazing at having a fresh, brand-new car. I headed to the salon and met up with Dionne. I went in and pointed at the stylist who had Dionne in her station already.

Dionne waved at me. "I was getting ready to call you," Dionne said, while Lana continued pressing her hair.

Soon as I pulled my purse from my shoulder, I plopped down in the chair next to her station. "I know. I saw your missed call, but I was driving over here."

Lana put the curling iron down and grabbed a cape to put around my neck, pushing the chair up high. "What are we doing today with your hair?" Lana ran a hand over my hair.

"I was thinking a simple updo. My dress is a creamy, beige color."

Dionne removed money from her purse to pay. "How are things with Khalil?"

"Good. I just left him at the car dealership."

"Are you excited about tonight?" Dionne asked.

Lana combed Dionne's hair so the curls bounced and took her cape off.

"I'm a little nervous, but he gave me a car, girl."

Dionne and Lana's jaws dropped open at my admission.

Dionne picked up her coat and moved from Lana's station. "And you still haven't slept with him, right?" Dionne questioned.

The loud chime of the door let us know traffic was picking up today. Usually we would come early in the morning to get away from big crowds. This place had a wax section and nail spot in the back like a one stop shop for everything to save time.

"No," I said and held up the keys to my new car.

Lana cleaned up her area. "Wow!" She slapped hands with Dionne in agreement.

"Do you think it's crazy to take a car from him?" I questioned.

"No. You can't live your life by what someone else thinks

or put a timestamp on your feelings," Dionne remarked, tossing her trash away.

"His family hates me though," I expressed somberly, crossing my arms.

Dionne popped a piece of gum in her mouth. "You're dating Khalil, not his family," Dionne's voice hardened.

"Exactly, if I lived my life by what others think, I would have never become a successful hairstylist and run my own shop," Lana reminded me of her being a single mother like me and having her own business.

"Well, tonight, we will see what happens."

"Anything from Jaylen?" Dionne inquired.

"He called to speak with the boys the other day, and they were in school. We ended up getting into an argument again."

"What do your parents say?" Dionne was sitting in the empty seat so as not to clog up Lana's area for her next client.

"I'm taking the boys over to see them this week. Have to let you know how it goes later."

"Well, just remember you're a great mother, and those boys love you," Dionne said.

I agreed, grinning at the thought of them wanting to get dressed up and go tonight.

Dionne was watching them for us at my place until we got back.

Lana removed my hair from my ponytail. "Let me get you over to the washbowl," Lana said, cutting our conversation short.

Four hours later, I was home. After getting my hair done, I headed to the store and grabbed something to eat. I arrived in my parking space of my apartment, and Dionne parked right after me.

She held the door open to get the boys and their bags out of the backseat.

"Mommy, I like your hair," Prince said. He dropped down on the floor, kicked off his shoes, and picked up his toy truck.

"Thank you, baby. I have snacks for you two, and dinner is already made, so Dionne, you shouldn't have to do anything."

"Mommy, can we come with you?" Silas asked as he tapped on my bag that held my new thong and bra set.

I dropped low to kiss them on their cheeks. "No, baby, this is going to be a long and boring dinner. You wouldn't like it at all."

"Is Khalil going with you?" Silas questioned. He went over to the toy chest and grabbed his action figures.

Dionne went in the kitchen while I dropped off my bags and got ready; it was going on five thirty.

"He is, baby," I called out behind my back.

"Here, boys, have some fruit and nuts to hold you over while I heat up the meatloaf," Dionne offered.

I heard them from the living room saying thank you as I laid my items on the bed and went to the closet to hang my dress on the back of the door. I picked up my scarf to cover my hair and headed to the bathroom. After a quick ten-minute shower, I came out and dried off, then opened the door to keep the steam from clogging up in the bathroom. I turned the little radio on in the bathroom and listened to Drake while I applied lotion and a little makeup primer. With my makeup complete, I was lucky I could slip into my dress instead of it going over my head. I walked out to the living room so Dionne could zip up the back, and the kids looked in awe at me.

"Mommy, you look so pretty," Silas said.

"Girl, Khalil is going to go crazy when he sees you." Dionne finished tucking in the slip dress.

"Thank you, Silas. Make sure you're good for Auntie Dionne now."

Right as I was about to walk back into my room, the doorbell rang, and the kids jumped up to answer the door. I yelled for them to stop and let Dionne answer it while I grabbed my heels.

"Hey, Khalil," I heard Dionne say.

Khalil responded, "What's going on, Dionne?"

I checked myself out again in the mirror and switched out my regular black purse for the short, white clutch. Finally feeling fully complete, I went toward the living room.

Khalil glanced up at me from talking to the boys and grinned.

"Hi," I said.

"You're beautiful," Khalil said as he moved around the boys at the door and closed the space between us to kiss me. I pushed gently on his chest, stopping him.

"I don't want to mess up my makeup, baby."

Khalil gripped both sides of my hips. "Shit, you don't need makeup, fuck that," Khalil said and tried to kiss me again.

I moved my cheek to the side, so his kiss landed on my cheek. "I care, and I don't want to be late."

He blew out a breath of annoyance like my kids did when they couldn't have what they wanted.

"I promise, after we've been there for a little while, I'll let you have a kiss," I stated and reached for my coat.

He pouted and kissed my hand. "Fine," he mumbled under his breath.

Dionne smirked, watching us. "Have fun, you two."

"Be good, boys."

"We will," Silas and Prince said at the same time.

...

I grabbed the champagne flute off the waitress' tray and stuck close to Khalil as he walked around and introduced me to everyone. The ballroom was huge with high ceilings. It was decorated with a white and purple theme with pictures of each award recipient hanging. The dinner tables had pictures of each charity helped this year. They had a DJ with a stage for dancing. The announcer said he was getting ready to begin the program, and we still hadn't had a moment to talk with his family because they avoided us. Lexi stood to the side, staring at me. I knew she was complaining because I saw her father rubbing her back to calm her down. His mother kept pointing at us, but I couldn't make out what the issue was. I thought I looked okay for this type of event.

"Having fun?" Khalil asked.

"Are you?" I asked, as we stopped at the table near the stage, and he pulled out my chair for me to sit.

"I only came because of the businesses represented in this room, on top of making the promise I would come," Khalil said.

"Is Kendall coming?" I stared up at the stage as the announcer cleared his voice to get everyone to have a seat for the program to begin.

Khalil held my hand. "Kayla was sick, so he stayed home."

The announcer held the mic. "Ladies and gentlemen, please take your seats," the announcer said.

Lexi quickly glared at me. "Khalil, you brought her tonight," Lexi said through gritted teeth.

"Lexi, don't start." Khalil tightened his arm around my waist.

"No, you're embarrassing me publicly with this woman," Lexi spat.

Being in public with all eyes peering down on us made me even more embarrassed and ready to leave. I figured we'd see them tonight, but causing a huge commotion and drawing eyes would make it worse.

"We're here to award some exceptional people in our community," Shawn, the announcer, introduced himself.

"Son, it's not too late to make things right with Lexi," Stella informed him.

I rose up and cursed them out, but Khalil put his hand on my shoulder.

"What I do in my personal life is my business, Lexi. Move on. I'm not changing my mind," Khalil told her.

Shawn continued calling out names and describing what each person had brought to the community. The photographers took several photos as they stepped down from the stage.

"Khalil, this is your family, and I would never come between you, but if they come at me one more time, I won't be responsible," I demanded, glaring at his mother and ex-girlfriend.

"Little girl, I am Stella Harrison, the wife of Samuel Harrison. Learn some respect before we have you kicked out of here," Stella argued.

I jumped up fast again, and my chair fell backwards as I pointed in her face. "Don't you ever disrespect me again. I might not have the money or last name like you, but I will be respected. Your son is the one who won't leave me alone."

Khalil tried to grab me back. "Serena," Khalil called my name, stepping in front of me.

I held a hand up to cut him off. "No, she needs to put her anger on the right person. I don't care about your money."

"Please.... girls like you only want to come up when they marry a rich man." Lexi grimaced, voice firm.

"That's where you're wrong. I've never asked him for anything."

Lexi swallowed hard, lifting her chin, her body met my eyes. "So, how did you get a new car that cost way more than what you can afford?" Lexi questioned.

"How do you know about the car?" Khalil asked, and Lexi looked at his mother.

"I have people everywhere who keep me updated about you, son," Stella said.

"You're spying on me!" Khalil shouted, and the entire room went silent and peered at us.

I felt so embarrassed. I snatched up my purse and stormed out as Khalil argued back and forth with his parents. I went out to the valet and asked for a taxi. Two minutes later, one pulled up, and I hopped inside right as the rain poured down. My phone rang, and I saw Khalil's name come across. I was pissed off that I let him take me there. I knew I shouldn't have run away, but I was ready to slap Lexi upside the head.

I answered my phone.

"Where are you?" Khalil wondered.

I bit down hard on my lower lip. "Heading home."

"I'll be there soon," Khalil said.

"Khalil." I felt myself irritated by his tone.

"Serena, I'm done fighting with you and everyone else."

"How is this going to work?" I said and gave the driver my address as he continued to talk.

"It will work if we keep outside people away from what we're building. I don't care what Lexi and my parents think. You are my woman," Khalil announced.

I stared speechless out of the window taking in his statement. "Okay."

"See you soon," Khalil promised.

10

—————

KHALIL

This was something I wasn't expecting, but the moment I laid eyes on her in the rain, I knew she would be mine. The way her skin glowed under the light as she lay across the bed in her underwear and tried to hide the stretch marks from giving birth. I smiled down at her and ran a hand across her stomach as goosebumps emerged on her skin.

"You're beautiful, Serena," I said as I bent down to kiss her stomach. Serena wrapped her legs around my waist. I wanted this moment to last forever, so I reached down to pick up my pants and grabbed my phone to snap a picture of her.

"What are you doing?" Serena cooed, lust filled her eyes.

"I want to keep this moment with me forever." I dropped the phone on the bed and hovered over her body, between her legs. I rubbed my index finger across her lips as we stared into each other's eyes.

She had curves more dangerous than any mountain road.

"Are you going to kiss me or continue to stare?" Serena questioned, reaching up and grasping my cheek.

I leaned down, brushed my lips against hers, and bit down gently on her bottom lip, pulling it into my mouth. I slid my left hand up her thigh and squeezed it.

She moaned.

I pulled back. "I hope you know there's no turning back."

"Stop talking," Serena said.

Easing into the next phase of our relationship I had to make sure we understood what this really meant. "After tonight, the boys and you are my priority. I want you."

"You're okay with taking on the role of father figure in their lives?" Serena's body molded against mine.

I wrapped my hand around her wrists and put them above her head. "I'm ready for anything," I stated, running my tongue down her throat to her right breast, then left. I circled my tongue around her nipple and softly tweaked it with my free hand.

"Khalil!" Serena whimpered, trying to free herself. Not wasting time, I moved down even lower and removed her underwear, slowly moving to open her sex with my index finger and thumb. I swiped my tongue top to bottom, and she moaned loudly.

"I will ask you again, baby."

"Yes... Yes... I'm yours, Khalil!" Serena cried out, then placed her hand on the back of my head as I dipped my tongue in and out of her sweet essence. She lifted her leg up higher, trying to push me away.

I smiled at the fight she was having with herself. I wrapped both hands around her waist and made myself at home with devouring every inch of her pussy.

"Khalil! Ahhhh... God, wait," Serena screamed.

"Mmmmm..." I groaned as I made small bites on her inner thigh as my palm ran smoothly across her stomach and waist in comfort.

"Fuck! Baby, you taste so good," I said. I pushed my boxers off and grabbed the condom from the corner of the bed. I slid it on, positioned at her entrance, and pushed slowly into her warm, tight sex. Overwhelmed, I shook my head, trying not to come too early, and pulled back out.

"Please... don't stop," Serena cried out as she reached out and gripped my dick.

"Baby, you feel so good. Forgive me if I come too early."

We both chuckled at my statement, and I eased back inside, stroking slowly.

"Oh God! Khalil!" Serena shouted as she thrusted upward.

"Yeah, just like that, baby," I coached as we both gave each other what we needed. I grunted and picked up the thrusts as the bed squeaked.

The kiss was bone tingling.

I felt the pleasure ripple through her.

"No more running from me," I demanded as I eased a hand around her neck, grazed my lips on her chin, then pecked her on the mouth. Sweat glistened against her skin, and all I wanted to do was stay buried deep in her soul.

"Shit! Right there!" Serena purred, teetering on the brink, then fell into impossible pleasure.

I pushed her legs back against her chest, sucking on her toes and fucked her until we both came and fell asleep.

...

The next morning I blinked my eyes open slowly to the bright sun beaming inside the corner of her bedroom. I grunted, not ready to get out of bed. I touched her side, and it was empty. I fully woke then, looked around the room for my clothes, and the door opened with Serena standing with a cup of coffee and wearing a robe.

Serena came in closer and shut the door. "Morning." She walked to the edge of the bed and sipped her coffee.

I raked a hand over my face. "Morning, what time is it?"

"Seven thirty. Your phone was going off, seemed important." Serena gripped the cup.

"Why didn't you wake me?" I reached a hand out for her to come closer.

She giggled and moved in, setting the coffee down on the dresser. "You seemed to need it more than me." She straddled my lap.

I kissed the side of her neck and across her cheek and chin as I eased my hand up her robe to find she was still naked. "You're wet for me?" I eased a thumb across her clit.

She gasped. "Aren't you tired?" Serena inquired.

Every touch was bringing up a new sensation for me. I knew just how to caress her.

"Can never get enough of you, honestly. But if you're sore, we can wait."

"I'm not sore, but I figured after going three rounds last night, you'd be exhausted," Serena quizzed and rotated to lie on top of my chest.

"You just awakened something in me," I responded before I pushed my tongue in her mouth.

"What about work?" Serena muttered, heat rushing up her face.

I squeezed her ass. "I'm the boss. They'll be fine. What do you have to do today?"

"I'm looking at the shop today to see about purchasing it and taking the boys to see my parents," Serena told me.

"Last night, I apologized."

Serena brushed a hand over my arm. "It's not your fault," Serena said.

The peace and quiet in the room and birds chirping outside made me want to stay in these moments forever every day.

"You're the best thing that has happened to me."

"Do you think they'll accept me one day?" Serena led my hand over the curve of her hip, to the juncture of her thigh and ass.

I parted her folds and plunged my fingers inside her pussy lips from the back. "I don't know and don't care."

She grasped my arm and squeezed her eyes closed. "Khalil, you need your parents in your life. That's not fair to cut them out." Her head burrowed into the hollow of my collarbone.

Need roared inside me.

"Let me worry about that. I can meet you at the first address, I have to go home and change first." I pressed a kiss on her forehead and left to go home and shower. My phone had a lot of missed calls, and the blogs had a field day with the event last night. My father wanted to talk, but I wasn't in the right headspace to handle them today. I needed a breather away because I was about to seriously cut everyone out who didn't support our relationship. I made it home in about forty minutes and jogged inside to shower and change. Serena texted the address, and I wanted to beat her there and have Kendall show up to get a feel for each place. I logged into a text thread with him.

> **Me:** *I'm meeting Serena to check out buildings.*
> **Kendall:** *Sounds good, bro.*
> **Me:** *Can you come to check them out?*

> **Kendall:** *I can meet you in a half hour.*
> **Me:** *Thanks. I'll see you soon.*

I sent him the address and removed my jacket and shirt, dropped my wallet and keys on top of my dresser, and picked up a fresh pair of boxers. I still had Serena's taste on my mouth, and I didn't want to remove it, but I had to shower and meet up with them. Edith was off today, and I had plans to bring the boys over here soon, so they could go in the pool. The water temperature was blistering hot, so I turned the cold water up a little to smooth it out. Closing the door with my head under the water, I thought back to our first sex session. The way she melted in my arms as her body adjusted to my touch. Everything about Serena last night made me want her even more, and I'd be damned if anyone stepped in the middle of what we'd built. I was never the type who wanted to be married or have kids but being in her presence and the way she was with her boys, I was more and more taking on a father role that I had no complaints about.

I finished in the shower and grabbed jeans and a gray T-shirt with my sneakers. I checked my phone again, and my brother was on his way to the first spot. I strolled out of my house when I saw Lexi's car pull up in my driveway.

"Khalil, hear me out." Lexi pursed her lips and fluttered her lashes.

I planted both feet flat on the ground and leaned against the car. "Lexi, what do you love about me?"

"What?" Lexi played with her fingers.

I cracked my knuckles. "Tell me, what do you love about me?"

"Khalil, that's a stupid question." Lexi thought because she was pretty every man should jump at her feet.

"To you, not to me though."

Lexi's shoulders slumped. "We're the same, Khalil; you can't ignore that."

"I haven't dealt with you in almost a year. You're telling me no other rich guy out there is calling your number?" I asked.

She looked away from me at that question like I knew she would.

This was a small town, but everybody knew how Lexi got down with men, and her father didn't care as long as she didn't embarrass him. It wasn't until I stopped fooling around with her that she thought it was a challenge to keep up the charade to my mom.

"I care about you, Khalil," Lexi said.

"No, you care about my money."

"My father is the governor. Don't fool yourself, you need me as much as I need you," Lexi spat.

"All you could do is be a piece of arm candy on my arm. No substance, and you'd never want kids."

"That's not true!"

I checked my watch and saw it was getting late.

"I have to be somewhere. Find somebody else to play with," I replied and walked to my car. I wasn't worried about her trying to get inside my place. The alarm and cameras would have the police out here in no time.

"Khalil!" Lexi screamed. She started up her car, and this fool turned, following me.

"Crazy," I mumbled to myself.

11

KHALIL

Trembling with anger I continued driving, ignoring my phone as Lexi kept calling me and driving erratic. I approached a light and stopped as Lexi honked her horn. I decided to turn right to lose her and meet up with Serena. Five minutes later, I ended up in front of the first building on Langston Street. It was two blocks from Main Street with the most traffic. Serena waved at me, and I got out to shake hands with my brother and kiss her on her lips.

In spite of earlier, inexorably, my mind returned to giving Serena my focus. "How many square feet is this?" I asked Serena.

The boys ran around in a circle as she looked down at the floor plan.

"He said it's about five thousand square feet. Do you think it's too big?" Serena asked.

"For cupcakes, it might be. Let's check it out."

Kendall opened the door, and Serena nudged the boys inside where they continued running around and playing.

I scanned the walls and ceilings. "How much is this place?" I inquired.

A little more construction would need to happen to update the mirrored wall and antique timeworn cabinets.

"This one is twenty-five hundred a month," Foster, the realtor I knew, said.

Control, I'd structured my life around that necessity in business and Serena being successful meant I needed to go harder as she gets started.

"How is traffic for this area?"

"It's a mixture; she would have the movie theater and a few clothing stores nearby," Foster remarked.

"For your first business, Serena, I think it's too much," Kendall stated.

I nudged her close to me by the waist. "I'm thinking the same thing, baby."

"Yeah, it's a beautiful space, but too wide open. I want something more intimate," Serena said and opened the door in the back room that led to the kitchen.

"We can try the second location on Main Street," Foster mentioned.

"Okay. Guys, let's go," Serena said.

"Can we ride with Khalil?" Silas held both hands up in the air in prayer.

Serena glanced at me, and I smiled.

"Yeah, can we, Mom?" Prince asked, backing his brother up.

Serena fixed Silas' button on his white shirt. "If Khalil says it's all right," Serena replied.

"That's fine with me. Let me grab their car seats first." I held the door open for them to walk out, and Serena grinned as I ran a hand over Prince's head.

They knew their mother and I were dating yet didn't feel any type of fear of having me around.

"Take care of my babies," Serena stated.

"Girl, we're just going around the corner. Calm your nerves."

"Mhmmm..." Serena smacked her lips.

She helped me get them situated in my car with the car seats, and I followed her around the corner. I hopped out to open the door on the other side, opposite of traffic. This place looked more inviting and since it was a few doors down from Inked, they'd get late-night traffic. Plus, all of the restaurants when people went out on dates.

"I think this is it." Serena clapped her hands together getting excited.

"Have you talked to Pops today?" Kendall waved me over to him.

The kids and Serena walked inside with Foster.

"Not yet. For now, I need space."

"I know they have their own way of doing things, but they're our parents at the end of the day," Kendall commented.

"Kendall, I'm not trying to hear that, bro."

"I know Mom is crazy, but if you do end up making Serena your wife, you don't think keeping the kids away will be punishment enough?" Kendall asked.

"Give me some time, man."

"You got that. I think she likes this place," Kendall said.

Through the open door, we could see Serena talking with Foster and pointing around animatedly.

"The spot is great and not too much to maintain."

It only took thirty minutes to come to that conclusion and see the way Serena lights up and was comfortable already showed me the future we are building together.

"How much is this place?" Kendall canvassed.

We walked inside.

"This is twelve hundred a month with utilities unless you purchase it flat out," Foster stated.

"I want it," Serena said, cool and gracefully.

The location was more of her style, modern and bright, cozy and more open in the space so she'd able to really fit her exact style on the decorations and updates.

"Then the lady shall have it."

"Awww!" Serena screamed and jumped up and down.

I watched her playfully dance with her boys in a circle. "We should celebrate," I said.

"I like that idea." Silas grasped both arms around his mom's legs.

Serena rubbed his back. "You two little bean heads are going to be ready for sleep soon," Serena said.

"We can just go over to Savory," I remarked.

"Kendall, you want to come?" Serena glanced at my brother.

Kendall nodded in answer.

"I'll have the paperwork emailed, and you can sign it," Foster said and shook hands with Serena and me.

"Thanks, Foster."

"No problem. This was the easiest gig I ever had," Foster announced.

He locked the door as we walked out, and I grabbed Silas and Prince's hand to walk down the block to Savory.

"I'm starving," Prince said and rubbed his stomach.

Serena cupped his chin. "Probably because all you've had today was cereal. Too much sugar and no food," Serena grumbled.

"Here we go." I opened the door for them to go inside.

Kendall followed.

Everyone said hi to Serena and fawned over the boys as we walked to grab a booth. Serena wanted to sit in a booth, and I wanted a table so we wouldn't be bunched up together.

"Serena!" a loud, husky voice yelled, and the entire restaurant stopped to see where it was coming from. A tall man marched toward us as I pushed Serena behind me.

"Jaylen," Serena gasped, holding the boys' hands.

I glared at him. I didn't care if he was her ex or not. I didn't tolerate disrespect, especially when it came to my woman.

"Come here, Serena," he demanded.

"I suggest you go over to your table with your girl," I argued.

His brow bunched together in a frown. "That's my girl and my kids," Jaylen hissed.

I got in his face. "No, actually, she's my girlfriend."

"Jaylen, you're embarrassing me and the kids." Serena planted a hand on top of her hip.

"Mommy!" Silas started to cry, and Jaylen started to walk toward him.

I pushed him back, ready to kick his ass not caring if I embarrassed myself in front of his kids. A grown man acting like a spoiled child because he never took care of his children or woman when he had them.

He caught himself before he fell down.

Serena tried to grab my arm, stopping me from punching him.

Kendall stuck his hand out in front of me to calm down. "Khalil, relax," Kendall said.

"Khalil, not in my restaurant," Wasim said, coming out from the back.

I balled up my fists. "Wasim, I'm sorry, but he came over,

hounding my girl." My eyes bounced between Serena trying to calm the boys down and Jaylen keeping his distance.

"I'm taking you to court, and you better pray I don't sue his ass for assault," Jaylen spat and stomped off toward the girl he was eating with. He grabbed her hand harshly as she tried to keep up.

I sighed and pulled Serena in my arms to apologize. Remembering the stories she told me of the way Jaylen treated her came back up again. I sighed and pulled Serena in my arms to apologize. "I'm sorry. I wasn't expecting to meet your ex like this."

Serena helped the boys sit down. "Try to not get into another fight in front of the boys again please," Serena requested.

I shook up with Wasim. "I will try my best."

Serena removed her purse. "We don't have a formal arrangement, I need to find a lawyer." Serena picked up the knife twisting it in her hand.

Kendall and Wasim spoke before he sat down.

"I can get my lawyer to find one for you. Don't worry about him."

"Jaylen will try anything to get under my skin," Serena said.

Already cynical and ready to find Jaylen, I had to make sure he disappeared, I wanted to change the discussion. "We can talk about it later."

"I'm not hungry anymore." Serena reached for her phone.

I reached across the table and put my palm on top of her hand. "You want to head home?" I questioned.

"Yeah. I can take them to my parents' house tomorrow," Serena stated and grabbed her purse and keys.

"We can get you guys some food to take home," Wasim said.

"No, thanks, Wasim. You've done more than enough with helping me out with a job," Serena said.

"All right. Well, try to not fight anymore today, man. I saw the blogs talking about the award dinner," Wasim reminded us.

"She's worth it, bro."

Regardless of the people in her family, Serena had only me to count on and she had enough stress raising the boys alone, so taking some of the stress away either with Lexi, Jaylen, or my parents was all I can think on.

12

SERENA

The next day.

"Uhhhggg... God," I blurted out as I stood naked with my back to his naked chest in his bedroom. He called me over for lunch, but we never got to that part because the second I opened the door, my clothes were ripped off, and he carried me up to his room. His arms came around my hips, moving up and down, then over my sex. He sank his finger deep inside.

"Khalil!" I whispered. In an instant, his long, thick girth hardened. I placed his other hand on the swell of my breasts. I felt branded by him, owned.

He trailed kisses across my shoulder, moving my hair behind my ear.

His deep voice sent shivers through my body.

"I'm hungry," Khalil said, his hands cushioned and massaged my ass.

I could tell it wasn't for food and the very air around me seemed electrified.

I whipped around, and my nipples stabbed into his chest. I lifted my arms around his neck and stuck my tongue in his mouth. "Make love to me," I whispered before pushing him back toward the bed. I grabbed a condom off his nightstand and ripped it open with my teeth.

"Let me have a taste first." Khalil's gaze stoked a gently growing fire.

I grinned and shook my head.

"Later. Right now, I need you inside me." Biting my lip, I eased on top of him, wrapped my hand around his hard on, and lowered myself down slowly. My eyes were closed tight as I rode him slowly. I slid my hands on his chest, moving back and forth breathily.

Khalil tweaked my nipples. "Shit! Serena, you have no idea what you do to me," Khalil stated as he claimed my breasts in his hand and sucked my left nipple into his mouth.

"Yessss... Khalil." A quiver surged through my veins.

He wove his hand through my hair and pumped upwards.

My breaths came in slow pants.

His mouth tugged at my sensitive nipple.

"The only ones who matter are you and the boys," Khalil commented.

I nodded in agreement. Having his mother not approve of me, and then Lexi popping in and out, along with Jaylen thinking he could win full custody, our relationship had been tested already, and I didn't know if it would last.

"Ahhh..." I cried out, unable to catch my breath. He was so deep, I felt my eyes roll to the back of my head. Every molecule in my body vibrated with excitement.

He rotated our positions, with him on top.

My mouth gaped open as he sank even deeper inside me, while holding my legs further apart.

I trembled in his arms.

"You belong to me," Khalil announced as he stroked faster and faster.

It took all of my willpower not to scream 'I love you' at the way he was taking care of my body.

He dipped his head lower to offer more of his sweet tongue.

I couldn't resist pulling him into me more. I felt shivers cascading all the way down to my toes.

His lips left mine to nibble at my earlobe. "Goddamn it!" Khalil yelled out.

"I... I... Khalil ... I'm coming," I purred and felt the heat of his body course down through the entire length of mine. The warmth and safety of his flesh was intoxicating right as I squirted and tried to cover my face in embarrassment.

"What are you doing?" Khalil asked before he moved my hand away and kissed my forehead, cheek, and lips.

"Nothing," I panted, shoving my tongue in his mouth.

He slowly moved himself against me. "Talk to me. We don't keep things hidden," Khalil stated.

I could no longer deny what we were.

"I've never squirted before and the one time I do, it's not with the father of my children."

"Who says I'm not going to one day be the father of the children?" Khalil retorted as he fell to the side of the bed and pulled me to his chest.

"Okay, on that statement, I need to get dressed and help the boys, so we can head over to my parents."

Khalil laid a kiss on my cheek, brushing the sweat from my forehead. "You want me to come with you?" he asked.

I rose from the bed, trekking to the bathroom. "If you can control yourself and not flip out." I turned on the shower.

Khalil came up behind me. "What do I get if I behave myself?" he asked.

I laughed aloud at his comment, pinning my hair up. "You get to sleep next to a warm body instead of cold sheets."

He smacked me on the ass. "You play dirty." Khalil cheesed with a smirk.

"Sorry, baby."

I combed my hair out and brushed my teeth. He wrapped his arms around my waist. Khalil turned me around, picked me up, and put me on the counter. Then he came between my legs, and I felt his girth poke at my stomach.

Khalil groaned nuzzling his head in my neck. "You would deprive me of your sweet... warm... pu—"

I cut him off with a peck on the lips and gently pushed him away to step down from the counter before we got into a sexfest. "We have somewhere to be," I said as I went to the shower and turned on the water.

Khalil smacked me on the ass.

I jumped and slapped him on the shoulder.

"What? I like when it jiggles," Khalil joked.

I shook my head and rubbed away the soreness.

He bent down and kissed both cheeks. "Feel better?" Khalil moved toward the shower door and stepped inside.

I passed the towel to him. "Yes."

He pecked me on the cheek, poured some soap on a washcloth and turned me around to wash my back and shoulders. An hour later, we were dressed and putting the kids in their car seats as we prepared to drive to Nashville to see my folks. When my phone rang, I saw an unknown number and decided to answer.

"I want my kids back with me, Serena. You're dating some thug," Jaylen spat in a gravely tone.

My own driving need to want my kids to know their father in the beginning was the only reason I fought so hard. Now after the nonstop cheating I came to the conclusion it was all a game to him. "Jaylen, you have lost any rights to tell me who I can date."

Khalil tried to take the phone.

I slapped his hand away.

His eyes darkened gripping the steering wheel.

"So, you think because he's the mayor's son, you have a leg up," Jaylen argued.

"Khalil has nothing to do with this."

Khalil drove my car since it was bigger and gave the boys more room to play. I made sure to put on their headphones so they wouldn't hear anything crazy.

"They don't even know me anymore," Jaylen said.

"Whose fault is that?" I glanced over my shoulder to check on the kids.

"You've changed, Serena," Jaylen remarked, thinking he could judge me.

"No, I've grown up and learned my worth," I fussed, hung up on him, and blocked his number.

"Serena," Khalil called my name.

I raised a hand to give me a moment. "I'm fine, just change the subject."

"He's only trying to get under your skin."

"I know." I choked up and cried at the realization that my life was moving in the right direction business-wise, but my personal life was falling apart.

Khalil took the exit that said Nashville, and I knew it wouldn't be more than four hours to get there unless we stopped for bathroom breaks. I already packed up snacks to keep the boys occupied during the drive. I felt Khalil grab my hand and bring it up to his lips to place a kiss on it.

I turned and smiled, leaning over the seat to plant a kiss on his lips. "Thanks."

"For what?" Khalil asked.

I leaned my head on his shoulder. "For not giving up on me and looking past my baggage."

"That's called being an adult, babe." Khalil peeked at the boys through the rearview mirror.

"Also called love."

"That's true." Khalil squeezed my hand.

My phone alerted me that I had a text message.

Dionne: What happened?
Nori: Wasim called Arvon.
Me: Jaylen happened.
Dionne: I knew he would squirm his way back.
Nori: I heard Khalil hit him.
Me: He pushed him, but Wasim stopped it before it got far.
Nori: Do you need us to come over?
Dionne: I'm always down to kick his ass.
Me: Lol! Dionne, sit your butt down.
Nori: She's already said we should start an I hate Jaylen group.
Dionne: Damn right.
Me: I'm not worried about Jaylen.
Nori: What about custody arrangements?
Me: He threatened to take me to court.
Dionne: He barely took care of the boys when you guys lived together.
Me: I know.
Nori: Seriously, Serena, call me if you need a lawyer.

> **Me:** *Khalil already offered a lawyer.*
> **Dionne:** *He was going around talking about Khalil using you.*
> **Me:** *I just got off the phone with him.*
> **Nori:** *Well, we're here if you need us, babe.*
> **Dionne:** *Yeah, Serena, don't stress over Jaylen.*
> **Me:** *Thanks, guys. I'm headed to my parents now with Khalil.*
> **Dionne:** *Tell us how it goes later.*
> **Nori:** *We can go shopping when you get back.*

I closed out the text message and my eyes to get some rest before the boys started to fight and fuss.

I woke up to us parked in front of my parents' house. I stretched and yawned as Khalil got the boys out of the back-seat. I saw the front door open, and my mom stepped out. She held a hand over her face to block out the sun. I got out of the car, helped the boys from the car, and removed the popsicle from Silas' hand.

I wiped the excess from his lips and hands with the wipe. "Silas, you've had enough. Khalil, how many have you given him?"

"Only one." Khalil chuckled.

Silas burst out in laughter.

I popped my lips. "I bet." I gathered the boys to move forward up the walkway so they'd be out of the way.

My mom opened her arms, squatting down to hug them. "Look at my grandbabies," Mom greeted.

Silas looked at me and then her. "Hi, Grandma," Silas said.

"Hey, baby. Give Grandma a kiss and a hug," Mom told him.

Prince and Silas hugged and kissed her as she picked them up one by one.

I stood beside them. "Ma, this is Khalil Harrison."

She glowered but didn't say a word. "Silas and Prince, you're getting big. What is your mom feeding you guys?" Mom asked.

"Don't start please," I sassed.

"I'm not starting, but I'm wondering why you brought him here. I know who his family is, and I'm not putting up with any mess," Mom fussed, then turned to walk inside with Silas and Prince.

"Nice to meet you too," Khalil said, extending his hand in greeting.

A groan accompanied the roll of her eyes. "Well, did Serena tell you that we don't approve of her leaving the father of her kids?" Mom inquired.

"Serena's a grown woman who can make her own decisions." Khalil shifted his gaze to my dad when he walked in from the back.

"Grandpa!" the boys screamed and ran to my father.

"My boys. Look at you getting so big," Dad said.

Clara and Roman Dunn were the same as Khalil's parents when you thought about it, only they didn't have the money and status. In their minds, I should try to work things out with Jaylen and not mix in with the rich high-class folks because I'd only end up hurt.

"Roman, this is Serena's little boyfriend." Clara folded her arms and reclined on the sofa. My dad rose and rubbed his chin as concern grew on his face.

"Mr. Dunn, nice to meet you." Khalil extended his hand in greeting.

"Did you talk with Jaylen?" Dad wondered, ignoring Khalil.

His face fell the slightest bit.

"I did, and I won't discuss my ex right now."

"He's changed, Serena," Dad chimed in making the situation bigger.

"Good for him, but I've moved on. So, are we going to have a good time, or should we leave?"

"I only made a small amount for my immediate family." Mom jumped up to stalk off to the kitchen.

My forehead creased with concern, and I left the boys in the living room to talk with my mother. Despite the support in the early years of my relationship, I had to show my parents I loved them but would not let their bias come into my life any longer.

Mom sorted her food trays. "This is just like you." Mom shook her head, gearing up for another fight.

I met her accusing eyes without flinching. "Me living my life the way I want without your input."

"Ruining your life is more like it." Mom had a critical tone to her voice.

"I told Khalil that no matter what, his parents love him even though they don't support our relationship."

She furrowed her brow, alarm bells ringing. "And you continued to date him knowing they don't want anything to do with you." She clenched her jaw.

"Khalil loves me, and I love him."

She curled her lips in a frown. "All you're doing is confusing the boys," Mom responded.

Ready to move on to keep the peace I changed the subject to something positive and proud of sharing. "I'm opening my own cupcake shop."

"You could have gone to college and gotten a job that would pay a steady income."

"My dream is owning my own business."

She gave me a hostile glare. "A business that probably won't last six months!" Mom shouted and snorted.

I exhaled as my hands shook. "Don't bother finishing lunch. We'll get something on the road."

I made a vow that when my children got older I would never run their lives and force my own beliefs in how they should live or pick the people they date.

13

SERENA

The stove alarm dinged and she lifted her muffin to move the pan on top of the counter gathering her spatula and adjusted the vegetables in a new bowl.

"Do what you do best and run away," Mom huffed out, in carefully spaced words.

Silence enveloped us.

I reached the handle on the fridge and picked up a bottle of water. "Tell the truth. You're jealous."

Mom slammed her wood stick on the counter. "What?"

I gulped down some of the water. "I followed my dreams and didn't care about failure, even in my relationships."

She handed the platter to me to carry. "My dreams have nothing to do with this."

"But you probably never wanted to be married and have kids."

Mom cut into the platter pulling up some of the sauce. "That's not true, Serena."

"Then help me to understand all the anger."

"Are you staying for lunch or not?"

"No," I said and walked out of the kitchen. I motioned for Khalil to grab the boys from my parents, and we left as they stood calling my name. I wouldn't come back until they apologized or made some type of amends with me first. The disappointment I felt in my chest from not having my parents' blessing would only grow into resentment. My life was about being positive and raising my boys in peace.

Once we got home, the boys were already asleep, so we took them up to the bedroom, laid them down, and put the covers on top. I'd give them a bath in the morning and a full breakfast. We did stop at one restaurant on the way back and had a meal so they could stretch their legs before getting back on the road.

I kicked my shoes off.

Khalil climbed into bed behind me and pulled me into his chest. "Talk to me," Khalil whispered and kissed the back of my neck.

I scrubbed a hand down his arm, making small circles. "Are we being unreasonable about this?"

His breath came out in small puffs of cold air. "Do you want to end things?" Khalil reared back to stare into my eyes.

"No." I laid my head on his chest.

"Then we aren't being unreasonable."

"I know your father's campaign wants you with someone more polished though." The support from Khalil showed me I made the right decision.

"I don't care about that, and I don't plan on running," Khalil advised.

I turned around in his arms and faced him. A flicker of a smile graced his lips, and I brushed a palm on his chest.

"You and I against everybody."

"As long as I have you, I don't need anything else." Khalil's eyelids fluttered shut.

My hands outlined his brows. "Plus, the responsibility of caring for two boys. I want them to have a relationship with Jaylen once he gets his shit together."

Khalil grunted, gently scratching my scalp. "I support your decisions. He just needs to go through the right channels."

"Thank you, Khalil," I said.

"Anything for you, Serena." We fell asleep in each other's arms on top of the bed with our clothes on.

...

The next day, when I woke up, I called out of work since we got in late from Nashville, and I needed a day with my girls just to vent. I was in the mall with Dionne and Nori shopping.

Nori searched through the clothes. "What color are you looking for, Dionne?" Nori's mind was always lost in shopping and spending money.

"Maybe a black or red dress," Dionne said.

"Legend is taking you to what again?" I tried blocking out the conversation with my mom.

"He's going to some banking thing and wants me with him." Dionne grabbed a dress from Nori's hand.

I motioned to put the dress back on the rack and try something else. "When you two started dating, did you have conflict with his family?"

Dionne lifted a white lacy dress. "No. I'm lucky Legend's parents live across the country," Dionne joked.

I turned to face her, scratching the side of my nose. "What about you, Nori?"

"At first, I was a little hesitant with Arvon. He was a single father, and I didn't know if we were moving too fast," Nori responded as she picked up a red off-the-shoulder dress for Dionne to try on.

"His parents were fine with you though?"

"Yeah. Jeanette's a sweetheart, but you know we did have a little problem with the mother of his children at first." Nori's face held a marred expression.

"Ohh... Beth. Right, I remember that," Dionne blurted out.

"Yep. Don't say that name around Arvon though," Nori mentioned.

We moved further near the perfumes.

I tested one of the Chanels on my wrist. "Kind of the same as Khalil when Lexi comes around or I say her name."

"I'm so glad to not have these problems," Dionne stated.

I picked up two more navy-blue dresses and walked toward the dressing room, sipping on a strawberry smoothie.

"I can guess the worry line is that things didn't work out with your parents." Nori rubbed my back.

Time is the wind that blows down the corridors, slamming all the doors. Life is complicated enough and dealing with so many obstacles from people that are supposed to love us showed a different story.

"They act like I deliberately went out to get knocked up by a deadbeat man." The exhausted influence of my parents getting into Jaylen's ear made it harder.

Dionne stepped out of the dressing room. "Give them time."

"I told them I wouldn't bring the boys back over until they apologized."

Nori stood and tugged on Dionne's dress to flow out.

"You have to do what protects your peace, Serena," Nori said.

"I know, and I hate feeling like I'm putting the kids in the middle."

She wore her hair off her face. "Focus on your kids and make sure they're happy," Nori commented.

"You're right. Let's change the subject."

"I heard you found a shop next to Zymir's place." Dionne walked back in to change clothes.

I sucked in a breath. "I guess Arvon's aunt spilled the beans."

"She saw you guys coming in and out of the store," Nori remarked, chewing on her bottom lip.

Dionne tiptoed in front of us with her hands smoothing out the wrinkles. "How does this look?" Dionne asked and turned around, showing off her dress.

"I like it," Nori said.

I agreed. "Yeah, it's cute, girl."

"Let me try the red one on quick. Then we can leave," Dionne told us and walked back to change.

"Wasim said he's going with Arvon to Khalil's place to play poker tonight." Nori tapped on her phone.

"Khalil told me they planned this a few weeks ago and had to cancel last time."

She looked at me. "His father's running his campaign and talking about how he's looking toward possibly running for the senate," Nori said.

"I wouldn't put it past him, but Khalil wants nothing to do with politics."

"Okay, ladies, how is this?" Dionne questioned, showing off the red off-the-shoulder cocktail dress.

I jumped up and whirled a finger around to move in a

circle. "That one is really cute, and I like how it flares at the end," I said.

"With black heels that would really pop." Nori pointed her finger toward her shoes.

"I think this is the one then," Dionne said and swayed her hips side to side in glee.

We walked out with two bags each of clothing, and I decided to finish our girls' day at the spa, so Dionne could get ready for her event coming up.

I frowned. "I just got a text message from Jaylen."

Nori stood next to me. "What does it say?"

Jaylen: I spoke to my lawyer.

"He said he spoke to his lawyer. Which is funny because last time I heard, he had no money."

"Don't engage with him, Serena," Nori said.

Me: I did as well.

I slapped a hand on my thigh. "Too late."

Jaylen: You're going down a slippery slope.
Me: Jaylen, get off my phone.

"We're here!" Dionne clapped her hands, dancing next to us.

Dionne locked up her car, and we went inside the Willow Springs Spa. The receptionist passed us robes and towels. I followed them to the locker room to get undressed for a full massage and possibly a facial.

"Did he respond?" Nori checked as she placed her things in the locker.

I checked my phone.

Jaylen: I'm coming to your house, bitch.
Me: I'd love to see you try.

"Ma'am, what would you like today?" the facialist asked me as I lay on top of the table.

"Can I get the cucumber and lavender facial and shoulder massage?" I put my phone on silent.

Staff started to work on us and we continued to talk then moved on to getting our nails done and waxing. Then Nori passed us a glass of mimosas after finishing up with the sauna and paying an extra tip. The spa day went well, and we stayed for over two hours and then had lunch out on the patio. Dionne pulled up to Khalil's house around seven o'clock. The boys were with Dionne's parents since I knew they'd probably be smoking or cursing like men normally did at these setups. Probably would have strippers if they wanted to take it that far. I knocked on Khalil's door and heard loud music and laughing. Five minutes later, the door opened, and Wasim stood there with a cigar in his mouth.

14

KHALIL

Serena hugged Wasim and walked inside, waving at everybody as I dealt the next hand. I needed a guys' night, so I called my friends over to chill with me since our women were out together. I even had Legend come over. He was Dionne's boyfriend who I met through her. He turned out to be really laid-back compared to Dionne's personality. He worked in banking, and we had crossed paths, but I'd never talked with him as much as I had tonight.

Dionne held a drink in her hand. "Who's winning?" Dionne quizzed as she came behind Legend and kissed his cheek.

Wasim smoked on his cigar. "Arvon and Khalil," Wasim said.

"Did you check on the boys, Arvon?" Nori inquired and took a seat next to Arvon at my dining room table.

Arvon pecked Nori on the cheek. "They're enjoying themselves with my mom," Arvon responded, sipping his beer.

Legend glanced at Dionne. "Did you get your dress, babe?" Legend asked.

Dionne reached for a snack from the table beside them. "I did, and I can't wait to show you later," Dionne stated.

"Did you guys already eat?" I asked.

Serena smiled at me. "We had lunch at the spa," Serena told me, cupping the back of my neck.

Wasim placed his cigar down in the ashtray. "Serena, you should have made some cupcakes for us tonight," Wasim grumbled.

"Sorry, Wasim. Only paying customers and my kids get freebie cupcakes," Serena joked.

I took the back of her hand and kissed the top, grinning. "You know she found a building," I said.

"I know, and I have to part with the best baker in the business," Wasim told her, grunting in frustration knowing she was the best thing that happened to his business.

Everyone chuckled because we knew he'd still get orders from her no matter where she went because he loved her cupcakes more than anything.

"I'm not leaving yet. I still want to work some shifts," Serena commented.

"You're the famous cupcake baker?" Legend asked.

"Legend, you know I'm always bragging on Serena." Dionne sat on his lap.

"That is me," Serena said jokingly and sat in the chair next to me.

I dropped my cards, turned toward her, and lifted her chin to stare into her eyes. "What's wrong?" I asked.

"I'm fine," Serena said somberly.

Her spirits were out of tempo with the tense drawn face.

"You're usually not this quiet."

Dionne tossed her hand in the air. "Jaylen is what happened," Dionne blurted out, voice cold and lashing.

"You saw him today?" I questioned, ready to go handle him and change those boys' last name.

"He texted me again," Serena said and glared at Dionne.

Dionne flicked her hand, ignoring Serena's glare. "Don't get mad at me for spilling the beans," Dionne taunted.

"I just want a night of relaxation." Serena laid her head on my shoulder.

I put the cards down and turned her to face me. "What did he say?" A heaviness centered in my chest not liking her being upset.

"He has a lawyer," Serena responded, picking at the lint on her coat.

A cynical inner voice brought another question to mind.

"He'll never get custody compared to what you've done for the kids all this time."

Serena caressed my hand. "What if his lawyer says something crazy about me, and Jaylen lies?" Serena wondered.

Nori moved close to her. "If you need any character witnesses, Serena, you have us," Nori said.

Serena smiled briefly. "Thanks, y'all."

"I have some friends at the courthouse. I can put in a good word for you." Legend extended his arm around Dionne's waist.

"Between me and Legend, babe, Jaylen won't even get a chance to speak the boys' names," I boasted.

"You're right," Serena answered as she removed her coat and went toward the kitchen.

I followed her as she pulled a bottle of wine out of the cabinet and grabbed a glass. "If you want to be alone, we can kick them out," I said.

She smiled and took a gulp of the white wine. "I don't want to interfere with your guys' night."

"You're more important. Besides, I've already lost three hundred bucks," I mentioned, wiping a tear from her cheek.

Her eyes widened at my statement. "I bet three hundred is chump change to you." Serena laughed and poured more wine in her glass.

I took it from her and placed it on the counter. "Hey."

"Yes?" Serena cocked her head to the side, caressing a hand up my chest.

"Never let another man cause you to doubt me or what we have," I said and kissed her temple.

"I won't." She pressed a kiss on my lips.

"Go upstairs and sleep, okay? I'll be up there soon." I captured her lips, pushed her against the counter, and squeezed her hip bone as she moaned.

...

The weekend.

"Foul!" I heard my brother call out, and I bent over with my hands on my knees, trying to catch my breath. We hadn't had a Saturday midday basketball game in a while with our busy schedules, but I finally needed to get out of my head and play a round of ball with my friends. Serena was worrying heavily on my mind and heart, plus the boys. Our cousin Rich's friend Lonny held his hands up to pass the ball to him.

"Are you here to play or just hang out?" Rich joked, dribbling the ball in front of me.

"Fuck you, Rich," I spat back.

He taunted me with the ball.

"Rich, you know he's in love now," my brother stated.

"I knew it!" Rich laughed then dunked the ball in the hoop.

I rebounded. "Fuck you too," I barked at my brother.

"Who is she?" Rich queried.

I stole the ball from him, dribbling to the basket.

"She works at Savory," Kendall responded as he walked over to the cooler near the bleachers, wiped his face off with his shirt, and picked up a bottle of water. He motioned at us, asking if we wanted one, and I said yes. Rich and I strolled toward him and sat on the bleachers to recharge and talk.

"Does she have any kids?" Rich investigated.

I glared at him. "None of your business," I spat.

"Aw shit, he's all possessive now. She must be sexy as hell if you're not talking about her," Rich stated, holding his hands up in mock surrender. I flipped him off.

"Might as well admit it to yourself, you care about her as more than friends," Kendall said. He grabbed the ball from Rich. I leaned back on the bleachers, closed my eyes, and thought about how over the course of every second I hadn't been around her, I wanted to call her just to hear her voice.

"When did you know you loved Bianca?" I asked my brother.

"What is this, an Oprah moment or something?" Rich joked, and I faked like I was about to hit him. He laughed and pretended to run near the court.

"I knew I was in love when I wanted to make sure Bianca had a smile on her face every minute and every second of the day," Kendall remarked, and I rubbed my chin in thought.

"I never thought it was possible," I replied.

"What was possible?" Kendall asked.

"To want to love another person and her kids like they're

my own," I answered, and we stood back up and headed back to play a one-on-one game.

"You've always been the non-committal type. What changed?" Rich sipped his water.

I shrugged my shoulders then stood in formation to steal the ball again.

"Serena isn't letting me walk all over her the way other women have in the past," I finally said aloud to myself and learned the truth in my statement. She was a challenge but raised the bar in knowing she was a queen and deserved nothing but the best from me.

15

KHALIL

Two days later.

I watched Silas and Prince laugh back and forth about who would go swimming in my pool tomorrow.

"Silas, don't forget to finish your green beans," Serena said.

He nodded in agreement and picked up his fork.

"What movie are we watching?" I searched from left to right giving them my attention.

Serena invited me over to hang out since we'd both been busy. The boys had gotten closer with Kayla and my brother, so we turned it into a family night.

"Uncle Khalil, can we come back another day?" Kayla asked.

"You have to ask Serena; this is her house, nugget," I said, pouring more wine in my glass and Serena's.

"Auntie Serena, can I come back over again?" Kayla inquired.

Serena laughed, taking a sip of her wine. "Anytime you

want to hang out, you can," Serena mentioned, and the doorbell rang.

I jumped up to answer it. "I got it; should be Kendall picking up Kayla."

"I don't want to leave," Kayla whined.

"We'll set something else up," Serena answered.

I laughed hearing Kayla mumble 'Auntie Serena' as I opened the door, but I lost the smile on my face looking at Serena's ex standing at her front door.

"Can I help you?" I asked, keeping the door slightly ajar.

"I want to see Serena," Jaylen said as he tried to step into her apartment.

I blocked him with my hand. I wanted to kick his ass and make him disappear, but I promised Serena I wouldn't get involved unless it was absolutely necessary.

"Khalil, what's taking so long?" Serena interrogated as she walked into the living room.

"Serena, we need to talk!" Jaylen barked, trying to push his way inside.

Serena stood next to me. I wrapped my hand around her waist, pulling her closer to my side.

"What's this?" Jaylen demanded, pointing from me to Serena.

"None of your business. What do you want, Jaylen?" Serena asked.

Silas ran around the corner shouting. "Mommy, I'm ready for dessert." Silas excitedly rushed over to stand between me and Serena.

"Hey, Silas, want to go live with Daddy?" Jaylen squatted down to his eye level, and Silas shook his head no.

Serena nudged him behind her. "Jaylen, talk to my lawyer if you want to see the boys. I'm done listening to your lies," Serena stated.

"Serena, stop fighting me and come home," Jaylen said. He tried to reach out and touch her.

I slapped his hand away and moved Serena behind me.

"Motherfucker!" Jaylen barked, charging back in my face.

Silas started crying.

"Khalil, wait," Serena pleaded, pulling on my arm.

I cracked my knuckles, cocking my head left and right. "Get in the house, Serena!"

"You think because you got money, you can have anything you want," Jaylen instigated.

"She already told you to talk to her lawyer, so I think it's best if you get off her property before I call the cops."

"Serena! I swear to God, if you have that motherfucker around my kids," Jaylen complained.

"He's been more of a father than you've ever been, Jaylen," Serena replied.

He tried to charge at her, I swung and knocked him in the jaw. He fell down. I tried to pull him back, but two grown men going at it was too much for her to handle.

...

After Kendall broke up the fight and took Kayla home, we helped the boys shower and read them a bedtime story. It wasn't my first rodeo since I'd babysat Kayla plenty of times. It was extra rough trying to calm Silas down after what he saw. I let Serena shower alone because I felt she was still upset about me fighting in front of the kids. Now, I was waiting for her to come out as I waited in her bed, setting the alarm on my phone. The light went off, the door opened, and Serena walked out in a short, silk nightgown. If I didn't get inside her soon, my erection would turn into fucking blue balls with how sexy she looked. She picked up the lotion and came to sit on the edge of the bed.

"Are we going to ignore each other?" I asked, cutting the tension with a knife.

"I don't want you fighting my battles, Khalil. Bad enough I have to deal with your parents and mine," Serena mumbled.

I leaned up against the headboard. "Hey. Hey... Look at me."

Serena turned and crawled up the bed, getting under the covers.

"My job is to make sure no one hurts you. That includes my family as well. I don't care if my parents like you or not." I caressed her cheek.

"Khalil," Serena muttered lowly.

I exhaled a deep breath. "No, what did I tell you the first time?"

"That your job is to make me happy." She stared up into my eyes.

I grazed a hand across her cheek, bent down and got on top of her, pushed my boxers down, and lined up with her center.

Her eyes widened with false innocence.

"That means no one will ever make you feel less than," I told her as I slowly scanned from her eyes to her lips to her breasts. I wanted to keep this picture of us together in my mind forever, the way our bodies moved in sync as my pulse pounded in anticipation of feeling her warm, wet mound.

She raised her hips to meet my body. "Baby... Ohhhh..." Serena called out, then buried her head in the pillow.

A sense of urgency drove me to want to hear those words again.

"Ughh... Fuck! Say it again." I teased her lips with my

teeth, nibbling them ever sweetly before I nudged them apart to explore every inch of her mouth with mine.

The sight of her enjoying my touch was too much for me to stop.

"Baby... please," Serena groaned as she ran a hand up my back. She opened wider.

I felt my body tense up, knowing I wouldn't only want to go one round. I might as well text my assistant that I'd be late tomorrow.

"You like this?" I asked and pulled out to tease her pussy with my tongue. Her scent filled my nostrils, and I dipped my head to take what was mine. "Feed me," I commanded as I French kissed her bottom lips. I held a wild neediness to pleasure her until she couldn't take it anymore as she twisted and squirmed underneath my touch. I parted her folds and plunged a finger inside as her nails clawed into the back of my head.

"I'm coming again!" Serena screeched, her body squeezing me tight.

"Not yet," I demanded, then lifted up and pushed back inside, wanting to feel her walls around my dick. I leaned forward and drove into her right as she gasped, hitting her spot. I didn't want to wake the boys, so I covered her mouth with mine. Her thighs spread wide to me as her sex clasped fiercely around me. My chest rose and fell on ragged breaths as my strokes sped up again. I clutched her to me as I buried myself deep inside, and my body settled over hers.

Serena clasped her fists in the sheets, and that wild, sweet scent of hers caused me to grow harder again as my breath panted out. "Awww!" Serena cried out.

"Baby... Fuck!" I mumbled as I tried to keep my moans under control but being inside her trembling body was breaking me down even more.

She could barely breathe, her emotions choked out. There was strange comfort in keeping her close to me. I took the kiss deeper, overwhelmed by the sensation, pleasure trickled down along every nerve ending.

Our sex life was way more loving compared to what I had with Lexi. With Serena, I wanted to know if she was pleased and able to feel how my body reacted to hers every time. It wasn't just about an orgasm, and more on connecting body, mind, and soul.

Desire leapt in her vivid eyes. "Ughh... Khalil," Serena whispered and leaned up to kiss my sweaty chest.

Her spine bowed upwards as if a string pulled on it as she came again for the third time as I felt my orgasm pulsating. I trailed kisses across her chest when she slid her hand between us and squeezed my balls. That was it for me, and I came for the second time. She cupped the sides of my face and peppered kisses on my chin, cheek, and lips.

16

SERENA

A *week later.*

I held Khalil's hand in mine as we stood with a mediator to discuss me having primary custody of the boys. I wanted the official paperwork with me in case I needed to put Jaylen on a restraining order. Khalil made a few calls and got us an early appointment after the last fight with Jaylen.

"I know your lawyer has explained everything to you, Serena," Joann, the court-appointed mediator, stated.

"He has," I said.

"You'll have full primary custody and be able to make decisions on both children," Joann spoke.

"Will you send a letter to Jaylen?" My heart thrummed wildly.

She sloped her head to the left in my direction. "Yes, and since he didn't show up and no lawyer is speaking on his behalf, we can assume he changed his mind," Joann stated.

"Will he be restricted from the boys' school?" Khalil asked, which was something I didn't even think about.

"He will, and I advise you to let your school principal know who's allowed to pick them up or not," Joann replied.

"I have two friends who are teachers at their school."

Ultimately getting to a point of needing supervised visits for the kids, really showed Jaylen is not the person my boys can rely on fully. There was heaviness in my heart.

Joann passed the papers toward me. "Great. I need you to sign here, and I do advise about giving him supervised visitation," Joann stated.

"That's fine if it's someone you can recommend, and we can be there."

Joann explained, filing the papers up, "Jaylen will be under strict orders when the notice goes out."

"Thank you." Panic was rising within me on how he would react.

She sat back in her chair, holding her pen. "I understand you weren't married so no alimony support."

I raised up and filled the glass with water. "I don't want anything from him except to take care of his kids. If he wants to have an account to put money in that the court-house monitors, I'm willing to do that."

She nodded her head. "Then I see no problem moving forward with this motion and filing."

"Thank you for doing this on short notice." Khalil reached to cup my hand.

"Thank your father; it was his doing," Joann informed him.

I didn't know that Khalil went to his parents to help me.

Soon as I signed the dotted lines we left, and Khalil was talking on his phone until we got to the car. I stared at him in disbelief.

"What?" Khalil pushed the unlock button, holding the door open.

I cocked my head up. "You went to your parents."

Khalil scrubbed up and down my arm, pecking me on the lips. "I asked my father for a favor."

"What do you have to give him?"

"Nothing. He's dropping his fantasy of me going into politics," Khalil promised, face close as if guarding a secret.

"Really?" I asked, shocked. I was halted by the tone in his voice.

Khalil pushed back his sleeve to check the time. "We do have to go to dinner over there a little more," Khalil informed, putting the car in drive.

I rolled my eyes.

"I'd rather take my chances in the courthouse with Jaylen," I joked.

"No, you wouldn't. I'd end up kicking his ass and going to jail, so this was easier," Khalil remarked.

"Thank you, baby," I said.

He scanned traffic, easing through the light. "For what?"

"Sticking by me."

"Only the right thing to do when you're in love."

I pressed the radio on and put on low volume. "Where are we headed?"

"I was thinking we can get the boys out of class and take them to an early day of pizza and playing games," Khalil said.

"You're really enjoying this kid thing," I teased.

"Don't be mad. They love the kid," Khalil said and popped his collar bragging.

"Boy, please."

Khalil drove away from the courthouse, and I was definitely feeling a lot better about where things were heading.

"Do the boys know about their father wanting to see them?" Khalil asked as he turned the music off.

"I planned on talking with them soon, but things kind of got away from me."

Khalil gave a sidelong glance. "They're getting older, Serena."

I sighed and ran a hand through my hair. "I know, and I hate to put them in the middle."

The car eased into the parking structure of the school, and Khalil turned the car off and took the key out.

"Try to focus on the good things that have happened. Do you trust me?" Khalil asked, as he stared back and forth out the window. The kids were on rest break and playing outside.

"Yeah."

"Then we can overcome all of this," Khalil reminded me, then opened the door and stepped out to come around and help me out.

"Promise me something."

Khalil led me toward the entrance of the school. "Anything."

"Khalil!" Silas yelled from across the walkway behind the gate.

"If you're not happy with me, let me know before you cheat." My voice was almost an affront to the silence.

He peered down into my eyes then cupped my chin. "There will never be a time that I'll be unhappy with you. Get that out of your head." Khalil motioned for me to walk in first and head over to the office to sign the boys out.

I smiled, lifted on my toes, and kissed him.

"Hi, Serena," the office clerk said.

She sat at her desk, talking with another teacher.

"Hey, Lisa. I wanted to get the boys out early."

"Sure. They're in recess so you can sign them out and put on the visitor pass," Lisa told me.

I voiced firm and final. "Sounds good. This is Khalil, my boyfriend. I want to put him on a list of people to pick up the boys if I'm unavailable." The support from Khalil gave me a boost.

Khalil reached his arm around my waist, tucked me into his side, and kissed the side of my neck.

Lisa stood and walked to the file cabinet. "Wow! Okay, let me grab the forms for you to fill out."

People ran in and out of the office as the bell rang.

"Also, my ex doesn't have permission to get my kids."

Lisa pulled the drawer open, sifted through documents, and brought out what Khalil needed to sign.

"You sure about this?" Khalil whispered in my ear.

"Positive," I said and watched him sign his name under mine and Dionne's, granting him permission to pick up and drop off Silas and Prince.

"All right, you're all set," Lisa said and gave Khalil a visitor badge.

We turned and left the office through the side door that opened to the playground. I waved at their teacher, and she pointed at us as Silas and Prince ran toward me.

Silas looked up, our eyes met. "What are you doing here, Mommy?" Silas questioned.

"I came to take you and your brother out for pizza," I said.

"Hi, Khalil," Prince said, giving him a closed fist bump.

"What's going on, buddy?" Khalil smoothed a hand over his head.

Prince high-fived us. "Nothing much," Prince cheesed.

I chortled at him.

Prince had always been more of an old soul compared to Silas.

"We need to grab your bags so we can go," I told them as we headed to Dionne's room and knocked on the door.

She motioned for me to come inside, and I let Silas run to his desk to pick up his things.

"What are you two doing here?" Dionne stood to hug me.

I pinned her with a long silent expression. "I just left from talking with the mediator, and we decided to spend the day with the boys."

"How did it go?" Dionne inquired, sitting against the desk and tapping her finger.

I crossed my arms. "I have full custody, and he can get supervised visits."

"That's great." Dionne narrowed her eyes, clasping her hands together.

"Khalil, look at my drawing," Prince said and pulled him toward the corner wall of artwork.

"How are things with you two?" Dionne investigated.

I glanced at Khalil and Prince talking amongst themselves about his painting.

"He's great. I never imagined I'd be in a healthy relationship and have someone who supports me with everything."

"You deserve it though, babe," Dionne told me.

"Well, let us get out of your way so you can continue working. I'll call you later."

Silas passed me his Spiderman bookbag, as Khalil walked back over with Prince's things, and we left the school together as a family.

An hour later, we ended up at Pizza Breeze, a family-style restaurant with video games. Khalil was competing with Prince on the race car ride and Silas had me hooked on the dance lane. After ordering two large pizzas and large, iced sweet teas, we decided to work off our meal and let them run around and have fun.

"Awww, you beat me, Khalil," Prince said.

I sniggered at his little poked-out lip in a pout.

"Next time, I'll let you get a head start, little man." Khalil passed him the winning tickets.

"I can have these!" Prince said excitedly, showing his brother.

"Yep. Go pick something out that you can share with your brother." Khalil stood to watch him run off to the prize counter.

Silas stomped his feet. "Mommy, you're messing up," Silas whined.

"Sorry, baby, but I'm tired." I stepped from the dance floor.

"Are you ready to head home?" Khalil wrapped an arm around my shoulder.

I nodded yes. "The day has gotten away from us, and I want to soak in a hot bath and drink a bottle of wine."

"That can be arranged," Khalil told me, tugging me close.

"Time to go, Silas."

"Okay." Silas jumped down and grabbed my hand as we walked over to Prince, picking up the fireman truck set.

"Can we watch a movie when we get home?" Prince begged, playing with his toy.

"Sure, just have to take your baths first though."

Khalil held the door open for me, and I got inside the car, while he helped Prince and Silas into their car seats.

"Move in with me," Khalil blurted out.

My eyes narrowed in confusion.

"Huh?"

Khalil turned down the street, heading to the freeway. "I want you and the boys to move in with me," Khalil said.

"What about—"

He raised a hand, cutting me off. "The only thing that matters to me is you and the boys. I want you with me from sunup to sundown," Khalil spoke.

"It's a huge responsibility, Khalil, raising children compared to hanging with your niece."

"I know that, baby. I wouldn't bring this up if I weren't sure," Khalil replied.

"Your parents?"

"I'm grown, Serena, and no matter how much you try to bring up reasons to doubt me, I love you and those two boys back there," Khalil commented.

"I know, babe. I just worry you'll regret it, and I'm sure I'm obsessed with you now," I joked as I rubbed a hand on top of his thigh.

"We can be obsessed with each other. I don't mind."

Khalil turned left at the exit toward my apartment with my car sitting in the driveway. He slowed down and backed in, blocking my car.

I removed my seatbelt.

He draped an arm lightly around my shoulders. "Go grab some clothes for you and the boys. I want you to spend the night at my place," Khalil insisted, answering with a kiss.

"Okay."

"Okay?" He raised a brow.

"We'll move in with you," I said and grinned at him, as a wide smile crossed his face. I leaned over the seat and grazed his lips, biting the bottom one and pulling it into my lips.

"Ewww... gross, Mommy," Silas said.

I chuckled and pulled back. "Boys, what do you think of moving in with Khalil?" I asked.

"Yay! Pizza every day," they both said, and I shook my head no.

I tried in my seat to face them. "No, it means we move into his house and become a family," I responded.

"Oh," Silas replied.

"What does 'oh' mean, Silas?" I questioned.

Silas kicked his feet back and forth. "What about Daddy?" Silas wondered.

"Your daddy will always be your dad, sweetie. Khalil is going to be a bonus father figure in your life. He'll never replace your dad," I spoke, letting them both know I would never stand in the way of them building a relationship with their father when they got older. At the same time, I let Khalil know he had a place in our family.

"I like Khalil," Prince said.

"I like you too, buddy," Khalil replied.

"Then it's settled. Let me go in and grab a few things, and we can go to Khalil's house."

...

Two hours later, I had the boys bathed and in bed watching a movie since it was the weekend. I walked into Khalil's bathroom and noticed the candles lit and the tub sprinkled with red roses and bubbles.

"You didn't have to do this," I said, removing my dress shirt and kicking off my heels and skirt. He wrapped his arms around my waist and helped me step into the tub, turning the lights down low and putting the radio on slow jams.

17

SERENA

The touch of his hand ran up my arms, I felt safe in his presence. All the air expelled from my lungs in one wild gap. "This is only the beginning. Let me make you feel good," Khalil said and moved aside to hand me the glass of wine.

"You're not coming in?" I asked, my senses throbbing with the strength and feel and scent of him.

He shook his head no. "No, it's about you relaxing. The boys are good, and I'm taking a shower in the guest bathroom."

"I'll miss you," I said and pushed my lips out for a kiss.

He bent down and gave in, and I tried to pull him in more with my tongue as he groaned and pulled back. "Rest and enjoy your bath," Khalil said.

"Okay."

"When you're done, I have something else for you," Khalil stated and winked, walking out of the room.

I came out feeling refreshed and relaxed. I walked in his bedroom and saw the lights were dimmed and candles still lit.

"What's going on?" I took in the room.

"Come lie down on your stomach. I want to give you a massage." Khalil waved for me to come closer.

I hiked a brow up at his suggestion.

"No sex, baby, just a massage." Khalil's mouth claimed mine.

"Mmmm..." I removed my robe and lay on the bed facing the headboard with my arms crossed underneath my head. I felt the bed dip.

Khalil straddled me with both of his legs on the outside of mine. A few seconds later, cool oil that smelled like strawberries trailed down my back.

"Mhmmm... that feels good," I moaned, feeling his hands rub across my shoulders.

"I knew you were tense."

"Yeah, with everything dealing with the kids and then the business."

"Now, you have me to help you," Khalil commented, and his phone rang.

"You can get that. It could be business."

"They know unless it's an emergency, not to call me after a certain time," Khalil said.

The phone rang a second time and then vibrated.

"I think I'm about to go to sleep."

"Good, and in the morning, I'll make a big breakfast for us, and we can go in the pool," Khalil stated and moved his hands to my lower back.

I grunted in relief as his magical hands took all the stress away. "You should start your own massage business."

He chuckled, and then my phone vibrated. I didn't think we'd get any alone time tonight.

"I think we're both popular tonight," I said, and he tapped me on the ass gently to turn over. I wasn't wearing any underwear, and his will not to have sex was killing me.

"Thank you for tonight."

"You're welcome," Khalil said, then lifted my left arm and massaged from the top of my shoulder down to my fingers.

Another thirty minutes went by, and I dozed off, only to be awakened by someone arguing downstairs. I jumped up and grabbed my robe and house slippers to make sure the boys didn't wake. After checking on them and closing the door tight, I walked downstairs to see Lexi pointing a finger at Khalil.

"You've lost the last little bit of your mind, Lexi," Khalil harshly spoke.

I awkwardly cleared my throat. "Khalil, what's going on?"

Khalil kissed me on the forehead. "It's fine, babe. Go back to bed."

"Are you kidding me! She's sleeping here?" Lexi argued, clenching her teeth, she was furious.

"Lower your motherfucking voice," Khalil gritted through clenched teeth.

Lexi pointed at me. "I will not," Lexi seethed and tried to maneuver around Khalil to hit me.

"I may be of a lower class in your eyes, but I will kick your ass," I spat and tried to move around Khalil.

"Baby, don't let her take you there." Khalil cupped both sides of my face.

Her nostrils flared with fury. "Khalil, you've embarrassed me for the last time. I'm demanding you kick this woman out, and we get engaged," Lexi told him.

"That won't happen because she lives here now, along

with her two boys," Khalil responded, and Lexi's eyes burned with envy.

"You need to leave." My tone was relatively civil in spite of my anger.

She shook with impotent rage. "I'm leaving, but we both know Khalil will be back," Lexi spat.

"I doubt that. Serena is all the woman I need," Khalil informed her and hugged me close to his chest.

Lexi rolled her eyes as she stalked out of his front foyer and slammed his door.

I swallowed the lump that lingered in my throat. "I hope the boys didn't hear that."

"Sorry about this," Khalil said.

"You can't control crazy."

He pulled me close, kissing my cheek. "My dad called earlier to warn me that she was coming over."

"When you were giving me a massage?" I questioned.

"Yeah."

"Maybe she should go on one of those dating shows to find a rich man," I joked.

"Shit! I doubt any man would want her. In her mind, she's everything a man would want: looks, money, and a cute shape," Khalil stated.

"That's not what guys want?" I asked as he propped his hands on my hips while I shifted to face him.

"Some guys, but not me. I need a woman with goals, one I can hold a conversation with from everything about the environment to business and politics. Not just always shopping and having meaningless sex when you can't stimulate my mind," Khalil explained as he turned the light off in the living room and turned the alarm back on as we walked back to his bed.

"Duly noted," I teased and pecked his cheek.

...

The weekend finally came upon us, and I had the kitchen full of recipes and the music blasting as I sorted samples for everyone to try for my grand opening. Dionne, Nori, and Kendall's wife Bianca came over to help me pick out a menu for our first day. I planned to bake at least one to two thousand cupcakes for the first day in case I got bulk orders. I carried the tray with twelve different samples in my hand and walked into the living room with the girls sitting and laughing.

"All right, ladies, here's the first batch," I said and passed the plates around.

"I saved my entire day for this," Dionne said, rubbing her hands together.

"Good, because I want this to be perfect."

Bianca stared at the table. "What are the flavors?" Bianca asked.

I pointed at each one. "The first batch is coconut cream, chocolate-hazelnut, and strawberry banana."

"I'm glad I got my workout in for the week," Nori jested.

"Me too, because you three will be my test dummies going forward."

"I want to feel offended, but the cupcake is so good, I can't argue back," Dionne joked and licked the residue of the chocolate off her finger.

"Dionne, are we still planning the party?" Bianca questioned.

Dionne nodded her head in answer. "Yep. It's going to be simple yet classy," Dionne said.

"How many invites do you have? You know the place isn't huge," I replied and passed them the second batch.

Bianca sipped on her water. "I like the strawberry one."

Bianca wiped her hands clean then picked up a different one.

"The second batch is lemon tart, the most famous of them all, and then cinnamon almond."

"I talked to Kendall, and he told me the square footage. Don't you worry, we got this." Dionne danced in her seat, tasting another cupcake.

"So, everything went well at the courthouse?" Nori inquired.

"Yeah, I'm so glad that's over, and I can relax now that I have the official documents." I appreciated their views and knew their support would help me in the long run.

Bianca's mouth pulled into a sour grin. "Has he come around lately?" Bianca wondered.

I wrote down their statements on each item. "Not since last time and no phone calls."

"Maybe he got the point this time," Dionne said.

Nori covered her mouth to eat another piece of strawberry. "What about your parents?" Nori snapped her fingers.

"They called a few times, but I haven't replied yet."

Dionne clapped her hands. "It's time for healing. See, what they know is that you've proven you don't need them." Dionne stood to grab the pitcher of water.

"I'll think about it."

"Any other news you want to tell us?" Nori smirked at me.

I felt my face split in a wide grin. "No."

"Come on now. Kendall told me you're living here now," Bianca said.

"I mean it's only been a day. I only have a few things here."

"You deserve this though," Dionne stated.

"Thanks, friend."

"She's right. I remember the nerves I had when Arvon asked me to move in with him and the boys," Nori reminded us.

"Any relationship is going to have its up and downs. You have to communicate and make sure to keep everyone out of your business." Bianca pushed her hair back.

"That's easier said than done. His parents and mine both hate our relationship," I muttered.

"At one point, I wanted to leave Kendall because of his parents. We separated for a few days," Bianca blurted out.

"What happened?" Dionne asked.

"A long story but let me just say that his parents are a piece of work. Unless you come from a certain status, you're looked down upon, and I didn't want my child being around that type of environment," Bianca spoke.

"And what did Kendall say?"

"At first, he wanted me to ignore his parents, and I tried, but they tried to play him against me," Bianca replied.

"Wow," Dionne said.

"They wanted him to follow in politics, and he refused. But he still let them dictate his love life until I put my foot down," Bianca said, drinking a glass of champagne.

I jumped up and headed to grab more napkins. "You have to do what's best for you and your child. I don't blame you," I replied.

"Ladies, how's it going in here?" Khalil strolled into the living room.

"Hey, Khalil," all of the women said.

"Hey, ladies." Khalil's mouth curved into a smile. "Babe, I have to head to the office quick to sign some paperwork." Khalil kissed me on the side of my forehead.

"Do you want me to leave you some cupcakes?" I asked.

Khalil rubbed a hand down his stomach. "No, I'm still full from breakfast," Khalil stated.

I pressed a kiss to his lips. "Be safe and call me when you're on your way home."

Khalil smoothly twirled me around and dipped me as though we were dancing.

"Awww. You guys are so cute. I can't wait for you to have more kids," Dionne mentioned.

"See? Now you're talking crazy," I joked as I walked out of the living room with the tray of cupcakes and refilled them with more samples. The kids walked inside with towels wrapped around themselves from the pool and Edith behind them.

"Can I have a cupcake?" Kayla asked.

"Sure, Kayla," I said and handed her a small piece.

"Edith, I made some burgers and fries for the kids if you can help me plate everything."

"Yes, of course," Edith said and escorted the kids to the table.

I grabbed plates from the cabinet. I planned the rest of the day to be inside with my family, and no amount of drama would break this special day.

18

KHALIL

I lied to Serena about signing papers at the office. Well, I did need to sign off on some projects. But the most important thing I needed to do was pick up the ring I would ask her to marry me with. I wanted to show her that no matter what our parents thought about our relationship, I wasn't going away, and neither was she. Since she had a house full of people, I asked Dionne to step outside with me. At first, she asked if I cheated on her friend, and I said no. She relaxed afterwards, and now I was sitting in the front of my driveway, showing her pictures of the rings.

"This one is gorgeous, Khalil," Dionne said, admiring the picture of the heart-shaped diamond with ten carats.

"You think she'll like it?" I questioned.

"Anything coming from you she will love."

"What about this one?" I pointed at the oval-shaped, two-carat ring with diamonds around the band.

"Serena's not over the top. So, something in the middle of these two would be good," Dionne mentioned, and I agreed.

"My favorite is this one."

A classic round diamond with a cushion halo sparkled in the photo. Dionne's mouth hung wide open.

"This one for sure," Dionne stated and passed my phone back to me.

"Thanks, Dionne. I'm headed over now to grab it and then head to the office."

"Are you planning to propose today?" Dionne asked.

"I was thinking about today at dinner or at the grand opening."

"The grand opening would be perfect honestly; she'd never suspect it," Dionne said.

"Now, if she turns me down in front of everybody, I'm blasted in all the blogs," I joked.

"Love can be a funny thing," Dionne said nonchalantly.

"I have enough of getting blasted from my family. I'd like to keep some of my dignity."

"She won't say no. I can bet you. Just take care of my friend."

"I promise," I said and watched her walk back inside my house. I slid my key inside the ignition and drove off. I already had the jeweler at the store with all of the rings I had chosen; it was just a matter of me making the final decision and paying. Then I'd go to the office and meet Wasim and Kendall at Savory for a drink. Taking the fastest route through residential side streets to the shop, I cut my time in half and arrived in ten minutes. I parked out front and ran in on a tight schedule.

"Khalil, you made your decision?" Bodhi, the owner of Luxury Jewels, asked.

"I did want to go with the round shaped."

"Perfect choice. Let me clean it up for you and get you the paperwork," Bodhi stated.

I placed my credit card down on the counter and

watched as he pulled the ring out of the cabinet and polished it. Finally I was pulling up to my office in shorts and a T-shirt to sign some paperwork for another business venture.

"Khalil, thanks for coming in," Antoine said.

"No worries. Did the numbers come in correct?" I expressed.

"Yep. We're under budget and bringing in a higher percentage," Antoine explained on the structures of the mall complex I was looking to gain control of and rebuild. As I talked with Serena, it gave me an idea to purchase the building that would help small business owners get a leg up with lower costs.

"Great. What are you about to do today?" I asked him.

"I have nothing planned besides getting these papers over to the courier," Antoine replied.

"I'm meeting with some friends for drinks if you want to come," I said.

Antoine nodded his head. Usually, I didn't mix with my employees outside of work, but he'd been helpful and stepped it up after the Lexi situation at my office.

"I have them waiting downstairs. I can meet you at the location in five minutes," Antoine stated. I signed off on every document and initialed where indicated.

"Thanks. Let me get out of here before these fools call me." I shook hands with him. I walked out of the building five minutes later, hopped back in my car, and sped off as my phone rang with Serena's name. "Hey, babe."

"I miss you," Serena said.

"You sound drunk," I joked.

She laughed. "A little tipsy."

I slowed at a light changing. "Well, don't get too wasted now. I plan on making up for the other night."

"Mmmmm... I like that."

A guy speeding ran the red light, almost cutting me off, and I honked my horn at him as he cursed me out.

"What's all that noise?" Serena inquired.

"Idiot driver," I grumbled.

"Where are you?"

I blew out a breath, turning at a stop sign. "Heading to meet the guys for drinks at Savory."

"The girls are all passed out from eating cupcakes," Serena joked.

"They got a cupcake hangover."

"Yeah, and the kids are watching a movie in the theater room," Serena said.

"Do you need me to grab some more things from your place?" I asked. Hearing the lightness in her tone made me feel good that she's in a better place.

"I can do it later once the kids take a nap," Serena mentioned.

I made it to Savory and parked. "I'm here now, so let me get in here, and I'll see you later."

"Okay. Have fun," Serena said.

I stepped out and shut and locked door. "That won't happen since you're not with me."

"Awww, gas my head up then," Serena joked.

"Always, baby. Your biggest champion," I responded and ended the call, then walked in as Wasim, Kendall, and Arvon sat at the counter.

"Fellas," I said and slapped Kendall and Wasim on the shoulder.

Wasim turned to shake hands. "The women kicked you out?" Whenever we got together it was a good time.

"No, I willingly left. I had something important to do."

"Yeah, my little brother is popping the question." Kendall picked up his beer and took a sip.

"You're ready for that?" Arvon questioned.

"Are you ever ready?" I replied.

Kendall scratched his chin. "True," Kendall said.

"Long as you love her and the boys, you'll be fine," Wasim stated as he lifted up the towel behind the bar and wiped it down.

"She's everything I ever wanted. Hell, even when I didn't want us, she kept showing up in my space."

"Then it's fate." Kendall gulped his beer.

"You deserve happiness, man," Arvon expressed, sipping another drink.

Kendall extended a hand around my neck. "You want kids?"

"I'll take whatever she allows. I'm fine with the two boys, or if she wants more, I have no problems. Can I get a scotch?" I asked Wasim.

He nodded, turning to grab the bottle and pour me a little with no ice. I started to pull out my wallet to pay, and he waved me off.

"Lexi blasted you when she came in for breakfast with her friends," Wasim told me.

"She's miserable and wants attention," Kendall stated.

I stood in between everybody. "Was my mom with her?"

"Just her and two young women." Wasim handed off more drinks to us.

"Maybe she finally got it in her head that I'm done playing her stupid games," I said, gulping the drink down.

"Only time will tell," Arvon mentioned.

"The girls told me they went to taste test some cupcakes with Serena. You know I'm losing my best employee," Wasim argued.

"You can still get cupcakes, just have to buy in bulk," I taunted.

He flipped me off.

"We put in the groundwork on the shop this week," Kendall said.

"Did the inspector come yet?"

"Yeah, the electrician and plumber will be in soon," Kendall remarked.

Arvon peered at me. "Serena told me you bought her a car?" Arvon thanked the staff for the plate of nachos.

"I wasn't letting her ride around in that beat-up car again, just to get stuck on the highway," I fussed.

"Let me feel your head," Arvon joked, placing the back of his hand on my forehead.

"What's that for?"

"Trying to make sure we have the real Khalil here. Spending all this money on a woman and planning to propose is something we've never seen you do." Arvon wiped his mouth.

I grabbed a knife eating the fajitas. "She brings it out of me."

"Happy you're happy, man." Arvon extended a hand for me to shake.

We continued talking and joking for the next two hours until I sobered up and drove back home to a quiet house. I walked in the bedroom and found it empty. I then walked to my safe in my closet and put the ring inside. The boys were in their rooms playing video games. I jogged down to the kitchen, and it was spotless, so I decided to go to the backyard and found Serena sitting on the swing set.

I headed toward her, and she angled her head to the left, watching me. "What are you doing out here?"

Serena broke into a smile. "Trying to bring back the

memories of being a kid. My life has flown by fast," Serena replied.

I winked at her, caressing her back. "Time has a way of making you stop and think about things."

"The girls loved all the cupcakes, and we narrowed it down to ten," Serena stated, diving into her business.

"Are you happy?" I lowered my voice.

"I am, and I have some people I'm looking to interview for positions."

I leaned toward her. "Just remember to have fun; it's not always about the money."

"Coming from the millionaire." Serena laughed at her comment.

"I'm telling you from experience, baby. Money can't bring you happiness. Enjoy these moments." I motioned around the backyard, taking in the peace and quiet.

"How are the guys?" she asked, changing the subject.

I chuckled. "Drunk."

"You're a mess." Serena playfully slapped me on the chest.

I bent down to kiss her lips. "Only for you."

"Let's go to bed," Serena said, grabbing my hand and leading me back in the house.

Thinking of the future, I felt I would have more moments with even more kids running around the house and us sneaking out together to be alone in the backyard.

19

——————

SERENA

F*our days later.*

"FUCK, SERENA," Khalil shouted, and I shushed him to keep quiet. Only a few times I gave Jaylen head, but we'd argued so much, I'd changed my mind and put him on restriction from sex. Dealing with two boys and working full-time had become too stressful. I kissed the tip of Khalil's dick, waking him up for the day. I stared at Khalil in bed with his eyes rolling to the back of his head as I moved my hand up to his chest while I squeezed and licked him from his base to the tip.

A groan started in his chest, climbing up his throat to spill out in a snarl from his lips. His mouth sharpened into a dangerous slash.

We were all moved into Khalil's house and were planning a big dinner with my parents tomorrow, so I wanted to put him at ease and please him since he was always spoiling me.

"Baby... wait!" Khalil's low groan left his lips, his eyes were demanding and passionate, hungry for something.

I always melted into the magnetic pull of his body and today, he was at the mercy of me controlling his pleasure. I pushed the covers to the side, climbed up his body, and kissed his warm lips, letting him taste our combined nectar.

"My chest is pounding, girl," Khalil said.

I chuckled. "So, you like it... Mmmmm," I said, easing down on his girth and rode him slow. His tongue eased into my mouth, and his hands gripped my ass, pushing in further, taking my breath away.

"Shit... I love you," I cooed, as I stared into his eyes and shivered at the heat radiating off his skin.

His teeth nipped at my shoulder as our lovemaking picked up.

"I want to be buried in this forever," Khalil stated.

I giggled at his statement. "What about food?" I raised my hips, turned with my back to his chest, and bounced up and down with his hand gripping my ass.

"Fuck! Keep going," Khalil said.

I zeroed in on his perfectly formed full lips, and his dark intelligent eyes.

"I'm coming, baby... Ughh, God." I tightened the sheets in my hand and concentrated on bringing us to the brink as a knock came at the door.

"Mommy, food is ready," Prince called out.

I tried to get off Khalil, but he held me down around my waist.

"Stop moving," Khalil said.

"Baby, he's knocking at the door." I laughed as Khalil

continued moving upward. He wrapped his hands around the back of my hair, pulled me back, and turned to kiss me.

"Khalil! Are you coming?" Prince questioned.

"Yeah, buddy. Give me a second. Go downstairs and get the cereal bowls ready," Khalil said, before he rotated us and lay between my legs.

"Really, Khalil?"

"Baby, you woke up the beast. I can't help it." Khalil pushed my left leg around his waist and trailed kisses over my breasts. He pushed back inside as I writhed under his weight and groaned as he glided his hands up all over my body.

"Yes... Ummhmm... Khalil," I moaned as I arched off the bed into his deep strokes. He circled his hips, grunted, sinking deeper and touching my spot.

"Arghh... Shit!" Khalil shouted as he came right after me. I smiled as he fell on top of me, still buried inside. I kissed across his forehead. "We need to go downstairs for breakfast," I told him. He rolled over on his back, catching his breath. I had to go to the shop and make sure everything was working well and then find something for the boys to wear to the party. Dionne was planning the grand opening party, and I wanted to make sure everything was perfect. I had lunch plans with her and Nori to catch up since we hadn't had time to talk.

"Why do we have to get out of bed? Let's play hooky." Khalil tried to pull me back to bed, but I shook my head and finger before running to the bathroom and locking the door. If I didn't, he'd be in here with me, trying to go for another round. I turned the shower on and pinned my hair up into a high bun as I walked toward the shower door. I loved getting to pick if I wanted a bath or a shower. Even the boys loved taking baths now since they had their own bathrooms, and they were connected together, so they weren't too far away from each other.

I was thinking about the amount of work I still needed to do before the opening, when a breeze from the door brought two big, strong arms wrapping around me.

I backed into his arms. "How did you get in here?"

"I picked the lock." Khalil's eyes glittered as they locked on mine.

I cocked a hand on my hip. "What! So, the millionaire businessman picks locks now?"

"Don't let the suits fool you, baby." Khalil winked his right eye, while smacking my ass.

"Well, I'm stepping out, so you can get ready."

"This isn't over. Later tonight, I want to have some alone time with you," Khalil said.

I stretched a hand on his shoulders. "Aww, do you miss me?"

"I'm not afraid to admit, I like having your attention," Khalil said.

"Well, tonight, I promise to give you all of my time after the boys go to sleep," I stated and wrapped a towel around my body to dry off and change into a pair of tights and a T-shirt.

Pressing a hand to his chest I walked down to the kitchen to the boys sitting at the island eating their cereal and skipping over the breakfast Edith made.

"Edith, you made all this food, and they didn't eat a thing," I said as they ducked their heads down low and laughed.

"Not funny."

"Let my boys have their cereal. Did you guys leave me some?" Khalil asked as he headed toward the island and grabbed a box of Cap'n Crunch, a bowl, and a spoon before sitting next to them.

"This is why they aren't eating healthy. Bad influence." I rolled my eyes at all three of them.

"Mommy, are you taking us to school?" Prince wondered.

"Yes, and then Grandma is picking you up."

"Yay!!" Silas said.

"What do you think of your new rooms?" Khalil poured milk in his cereal.

Edith wiped the counter down and handed me a plate with scrambled eggs, toast, hash browns, and sausage. I grabbed the glass of orange juice and took a sip.

"We love them!" Prince said.

Khalil handed them both a glass of orange juice. "Good, I'm happy," Khalil responded, kissing me on the top of my head.

Silas wiggled in his seat. "Can we get in the pool?" Silas inquired.

Seeing the smiles and busy morning we've created from this interaction felt like a dreamlike moment.

I cut into the sausage and eggs, spreading butter on my toast. "On the weekend, when you're out of school, and we can watch you both."

"What are your plans for today?" Khalil asked.

"I need to run by the shop; an electrician is coming. Then lunch with Nori and Dionne."

Khalil reached in his pocket and handed a credit card toward me. "Keep me posted. I'm headed to the office and might run by to see my brother," Khalil said.

I grinned, shaking my head at him. "I shouldn't be too late, so we can make dinner and give Edith the day off."

"You don't have to do that, Serena. I'm happy to have a house full here now," Edith said.

"Here we go," Khalil groaned as Edith hit him on the back of the head.

"Ouch!" Khalil shouted, and the boys laughed and pointed at him.

"That's what you get." I rose from my chair, put my empty plate in the sink, and kissed him on the forehead before walking out of the kitchen.

Prince and Silas hurried out of the kitchen behind me. They held onto their lunch bags, and I picked up their jackets from the coatrack.

"Be good today!" I called out as I grabbed my coat and purse off the couch and opened the front door to leave. They raced to the car before I could unlock the door on my new car. I hated to take it at first, but Khalil insisted once we made things official. Looking at all the mansions in the neighborhood in awe, never in my life did I think I would be living in this type of place with someone who loved me and my kids. I headed to the school and grinned at the two of them talking in the backseat. I pulled up to the drop off spot to let them out as I checked my cell and noticed a text from Khalil.

Khalil: *Have a good day, beautiful.*

I returned his text message as I stopped at the red light.

Me: *You too, and I'll do that thing again tonight.*

I teased and closed out of the text app, pulling from Main Street next to Jones, and parked.

...

That afternoon, I got out of the car and grabbed the paperwork for the plumber and designer. Picking up my purse, I strolled inside as the construction crew from Kendall's company took measurements for the bar rack. I waved at Kendall and dropped my things on the counter as he gave me a one-arm hug.

"How's it going, Kendall?" I quizzed.

"Everything is on track. We have about two weeks left, and then you should be good to go," Kendall said.

"Will we be able to fit to capacity with the double ovens and the section for the chocolate fountain?"

"Yeah, you have plenty of space. I think it would be good to add a section for kids, so when parents come inside to relax with a sitting area, the kids have their own space too," Kendall told me.

"I like that idea; will it cause us to be behind schedule?" I inquired.

"No, it will be fine," Kendall said.

"Sounds good. I need to get my office set up." I strolled to the back office, moving boxes around and putting up pictures I left from the other night.

I heard a knock at the door and saw Jaylen standing with his hands in his pockets. The last time we saw each other, all we did was argue, and I wasn't in the mood to argue with him again.

"Don't have time to fight with you," I muttered, hammering the nail in the wall to hang my picture of the boys.

Jaylen slipped his hands in his pockets. "Serena, I come in peace, seriously."

"I doubt that," I muttered and turned around to look at him.

"Seriously, I want us to get in a better place," Jaylen suggested as he swaggered in and sat on the couch in the corner of my office. I asked Kendall to bust a wall down to extend it enough so when the boys came to hang out, they'd have enough room to play.

"What do you want, Jaylen? I'm happy, and the boys are healthy and happy."

"I know you've had the burden of raising them on your own for years," Jaylen cited.

I blew out a breath of frustration and crossed my arms over my chest.

"I messed up everything, and I take full responsibility. I want to see my kids and let them know their brothers and sisters," Jaylen stated.

"You know I have full custody. I don't mind supervised visits on the weekends, and we can see what happens."

Jaylen rubbed his chin. "I can't argue with that," Jaylen mumbled, gazing around the office.

"You have no leg to stand on at this point, Jaylen," I said and answered my ringing phone with Dionne's name flashed across.

"Hey."

"We're at Jones. You can just walk over here if you're done," Dionne said.

"Thanks. Give me a second. Go ahead and order me a salad," I replied, then hung up the call.

"Are you happy?" Jaylen brought up.

"You don't get to ask me that." I rubbed my temples, not up to having another yelling match.

"I know, Serena, but I do still love and care about you. I admit I fucked everything up, with our relationship and then the kids. I always wanted you to be happy." Jaylen tried to reach out and touch my hand, but I pulled away.

I sighed. "Yes. I'm happy, and I have an appointment I need to get to."

"Sorry, I don't want your boyfriend jumping out of a closet on my ass," Jaylen joked.

"Khalil can be a little protective over me."

"Shit, he looked like a shark ready for his prey when I stepped within an inch of you," Jaylen commented, and I waved him off.

I gathered my purse and keys so we could walk out together.

"I will let you know when we can meet up with the boys. I have dinner plans with my parents tomorrow. Maybe later this weekend."

Jaylen marched down the hallway, and I turned toward the bathroom with the plumber working.

"Jaylen, I'll call you," I shouted out, and he motioned with his hand. "Hey, Dan. I have the paperwork on my desk you can grab. I'm heading next door for lunch if you need anything," I informed him as my phone vibrated with another message from Dionne.

Dionne: *Your food is ready. Hurry up!*
Me: *I'm coming.*

I replied as Dan rubbed the sweat from his forehead with the towel.

"Thanks, Serena. I'll have you up and running in no time," Dan called out. I ran a hand through my hair and went next door to Jones and saw the girls sitting at a table.

...

Dionne raised her hand in greeting. "You look cute, kind of glowing." She fiddled with her earring. The waitress came over and placed another glass of wine on the table.

"Drinking early," I sassed as I drummed my fingers on the table.

"This is her second one, and I'm wondering what the problem is." Nori crossed her legs in the chair.

"Nothing's wrong. I just wanted to see you guys and see how you're all feeling." Dionne brushed the creases from her jacket.

"You seem anxious about what's happening?" I asked.

"I'm excited about the cupcake shop opening and the party," Dionne replied. I took a sip of water and took a bite of the salad.

"We finally finished moving in with Khalil."

"That's great. I know the boys are excited," Nori commented.

"Silas has a Black Panther room, and Prince's is decorated in Batman."

Dionne set her palms down flat on the table.

"So, I have fifty guests who've RSVP'd for your opening. Plus, with Khalil's family name, a few photographers will put some photos in the newspaper," Dionne explained.

A smile parted my lips. "Seriously, the newspaper?"

"Yep, so get ready because you're going to be the biggest thing that hit Murfreesboro," Dionne informed me, as she picked up her knife and cut into her baked potato skins.

"Do you need me to bring anything?" Nori inquired as she darted her eyes from me to Dionne.

I pressed my palms together.

"No, just come with the kids and Arvon. I have everything covered." Dionne gulped down her glass of wine.

"How are things with you and Legend?" I asked.

"Good, he's excited about us starting a family," Dionne declared.

I clapped my hands in glee.

"Really! I can't wait to see you with a swollen belly," I joked.

"It's too early to start with jokes about a swollen belly." Dionne grimaced as emotions flitted across her face.

"Well, I submit my name as godmother," Nori teased, and I howled out in laughter.

"Shouldn't you two be working today?" I bit down on a piece of bread.

"We took a personal day so we could see you," Dionne said.

"Basically, you skipped class." All three of us laughed and talked for the rest of the afternoon, and then we headed out to shop.

Later in the afternoon, when I stepped inside the house, the boys were sitting on the couch under Khalil's arms, watching a movie. I dropped my purse and bags near the door, walked over, and kissed all three of them.

"How was your day?" Khalil queried as he stood and followed me up the stairs to the bedroom. I sat back on the bed, sighed, and looked up at the ceiling.

"Tired?" Khalil lifted my foot and removed my shoe.

"Long day of business, lunch, and then shopping. I'm wiped out." Khalil motioned for me to turn on my stomach. He raised my arms and removed my shirt and pants. I closed my eyes and felt his hands against my shoulders, massaging my back and thighs.

"I'll let you rest. Don't worry about dinner. We ordered pizza, and I gave Edith the night off. You rest," Khalil said, kissing behind my ear.

"Are you sure? I promised it would be our time tonight," I mumbled.

"Positive, just remember you need to pace yourself and not stress," Khalil demanded, and I turned my head, then lifted up for a kiss. He got off the bed and turned the light off, and I dozed off in a deep sleep.

20

SERENA

The next day, Khalil drove me and the boys to my parents' house for dinner. I tried to control the butterflies in my stomach, but the way we left things last time we spoke wasn't the best. My mom was always about Jaylen and me being together no matter what, so the boys could be in a two-parent household. I was determined not to let them run my life again and manipulate me into being with Jaylen. Khalil parked in front of their house, shut the car off, and gripped my left hand, kissing the back of my palm.

"Stop being nervous," Khalil said as he leaned over to peck my lips.

"Is it obvious?" I probed, checking my makeup in the visor.

"Boys, you ready to see your Granny and Pops?" Khalil shifted in his seat and tapped them both on the leg.

"Yes!" Prince and Silas shouted and clapped their hands together.

Khalil unbuckled his seatbelt, got out of the car, and helped us all out of the car. I had dressed them both in black shorts and their favorite superhero shirt since it was the weekend, and they could roam around all day until they got restless.

I grasped Khalil's hand and strolled to the front door, attempting to knock when it automatically opened with my dad standing there with a smile on his face.

"Look at these two big boys," Dad spoke as Silas and Prince ran into his arms.

"Hi, Grandpa!" Prince said as he wrapped his arms around Dad's neck.

"I missed you two so much," Dad muttered as he kissed the side of their cheeks.

"We missed you," Silas said, and I wiped a tear that started to fall.

Dad stepped back to let us inside. He shook hands with Khalil and pulled me in for a hug.

"How are you doing?" I probed him, looking around the house and seeing it was still the same.

"Working as usual. Come on inside so we can talk. Boys, do you want some ice cream?" Dad asked and of course, they screamed yes.

"Only a little bit, you still have dinner to eat," I replied. It was going to be six p.m., and they'd already been up all night for the weekend, and I planned on working at the shop tomorrow.

"Hi, babies," Mom said, coming into the living room.

"Hi, Grandma," Silas muttered as he ran into her arms. I knew they missed my parents since the first year after I left Jaylen we lived here together.

"The food is almost ready. Can I get you something to drink?" Dad inquired, and I said wine would be fine.

"Boys, go play in your old room, so we can talk with your mom," Mom said.

Silas and Prince peered over at me, and I nodded in agreement.

"Wow, I can't believe how big they've gotten, Serena," Mom stated.

"Two growing boys that drive me crazy."

"Khalil, I owe you an apology. Well, both of you really," Dad said as he passed me a glass of wine and Khalil a beer.

"Same, Serena, we were brought up in the old traditional way of having the father in the household, and we didn't look beyond our own selfish reasons," Mom stated.

"I talked with Jaylen, and he knows that we're in support of you two being together," Dad told us.

"I'm glad to hear that," I said.

"It wasn't right for us to try to push you back into a bad situation. We love you, Serena, and only want you to be happy." Mom extended her hand, and I reached over to close the space between us.

"I forgive you and want you to know that Khalil is the best thing for me and the boys."

"We know that, baby. We unfairly thought of you being your father's son, and neither his nor your mother's reputation are the best," Mom voiced.

"I understand, and believe me, I wasn't trying to live in their shadow growing up," Khalil commented.

"Well, let's start fresh and get to know each other better," Mom said as she put her arm around my shoulder. We headed into the kitchen to eat, and I noticed all of my favorites: cabbage, sweet potatoes, cornbread, spaghetti, and beef stroganoff.

"Wow! I wasn't expecting all this food."

"You can take some home," Mom offered as she motioned for us to take a seat.

My dad came into the room with the boys holding their toys in both hands.

"I knew it wouldn't last long until you got into some toys. Put them back in the room so we can eat."

"Aww, Mom," Prince soberly said.

"Don't 'aww Mom' me. You already had ice cream and now toys."

"Listen to your mom, Prince. After we get home, we can play video games," Khalil announced, and they excitedly dropped the toys right on the floor and hopped into their seats.

"See, he has them spoiled rotten."

"Not just them," Khalil teased as he leaned over to capture my lips.

"Just like your father," Mom told him.

"How is work going at the restaurant?" Dad inquired.

"I quit Savory a few weeks ago. I'm focused on getting the bakery open full-time," I explained.

"You finally opened the bakery?" Mom investigated while she filled Silas' plate with cabbage and then Prince's.

"The construction is halfway done. We're having a grand opening party if you want to come," I invited them.

"We'd love to come to support you," Dad insisted.

"I talked with Jaylen yesterday," I announced, and the room went silent.

"When did that happen?" Khalil probed.

"He came to the shop."

"Did he hurt you?" Khalil questioned.

"No, he came in humble and asked if he could see the boys. I told him supervised and on the weekends."

"He's remarried right?" Mom grilled.

"Yeah, with two kids. I told him all I ever wanted was for him to have a relationship with the kids."

"I think you did the right thing not holding grudges," Mom said.

"It took awhile to get here, but I'm in a good space and only want peace in my life."

Khalil slid his hand on top of my palm and squeezed. I smiled and continued talking about the shop.

We ended up talking longer and taking pictures with my parents, then playing board games. We finally made it home before midnight and tucked the boys in bed. Khalil was taking us over to his parents' house next, and I hoped things went as smooth as they did today. I shut the TV off and pulled the covers up over my shoulders as Khalil finished a text on his phone.

"Tired?" Khalil investigated as he ran a hand across my back, while I yawned and stretched my arms.

"Exhausted. How are you feeling about my parents?"

"The question is what do you think? I'm on your side no matter what." Khalil turned to his side and faced me.

"Glad the kids get to be in their lives, and they apologized. Hopefully, in time we'll see."

"Have I told you lately I'm happy you moved in here with me?" Khalil spoke, his voice quiet yet intense.

"I had no choice with the way you were stuck up under me," I joked.

"Woman, you have no idea how stuck I want to be with you." Khalil bit down on my shoulder in a joking manner.

"Stop, you're going to wake the boys. You know how you get."

"I'm not the only one who's out here crying and moaning out loud," Khalil taunted as he fanned himself.

"I do not act like that. Take it back." I punched him in the arm lightly.

"I love hearing your moans, whimpering, and seeing

your facial expressions when I first push inside your tight, warm pussy," Khalil groaned as he rubbed his palm up and down my arm.

"Thank you, baby, but I'm going to bed. We have another busy day tomorrow."

"Fine, but it's going to be hard sleeping next to you in nothing but those little ass shorts," Khalil suggested.

I giggled at him, ran a hand up his chest, and patted his cheek. Khalil turned the light off and pulled me into his side. I fell asleep listening to his heartbeat.

...

Today was a brand-new day. We woke up and got the boys up to eat breakfast and then took them over to see the shop. I had them inside helping me paint a little until it was time for lunch with Khalil's parents. I checked to make sure Prince was rolling the brush correctly, and he accidentally got a little on his shoes.

"How does it look, Mommy?" Silas called out, pointing at his section of the wall.

I gripped his shoulder. "I love it." Suddenly, I got emotional even more knowing we were building something together. Years from now they can look back and know how much time and love went into our family business. "It looks good, baby boy," I expressed to Prince.

Dionne walked inside holding smoothies and passed one to me and then the boys. "Here's your pick-me-up," Dionne said.

"I love this off-white cream color. Kendall is putting in a chocolate bar, and a section for the kids," I explained.

"How many tables will you have?" Dionne wondered.

"Prince, slow down on that smoothie," I spoke then watched him drop the paintbrush and drink his smoothie.

"Okay," Prince said.

"I'll have about six or seven tables. I want it more for people to come in and out unless they have kids."

"That'll be cute. How did dinner go with your parents?" Dionne interrogated.

I dropped my brush and strolled to my office with Dionne behind me.

"Khalil, can you watch them please?"

He nodded in agreement, and I opened the door to my office and walked around to my desk.

"What's wrong?" Dionne grilled.

"I'm nervous about meeting his parents again."

"You're dating Khalil, not his parents," Dionne said.

"I know, but they're his parents. What if some time down the road he wants a relationship with them, and I was the cause of them being apart?"

"You can't worry about that. The most important thing is you and the boys. Khalil loves you," Dionne stated.

"I know and I love him, but I'm not sure if they'll like me."

"Well, I think you need to just focus on making sure Khalil is happy and forget about making his crazy mother happy." Dionne tossed her smoothie in the trash can.

I checked the time on my watch and noticed we needed to get going. "I have to get the boys cleaned up so we can go."

"Do you want me to go with you guys?" Dionne questioned.

I cleaned up some of the mess, tossing it in the trash bin. "No, the last thing I need is you fighting with his parents."

"Did Nori tell you if she's coming to the grand opening?" Dionne checked.

"She texted that she was coming with Arvon and the boys."

"Perfect! I'm so excited for you. I have a DJ and all the works planned," Dionne excitedly said.

"Are we still on track with the budget?"

"Khalil took care of the money, don't worry." Dionne stood.

I jumped up as well to follow behind to the front. "I told you to let me know if you needed anything."

"And I will, but Khalil wants your grand opening to be special. So, let the man do something nice for you," Dionne demanded.

"Are you ready to go?" Khalil wanted to know, grabbing his keys from his pocket.

"I need to get the boys cleaned up. Do you think we have time to get them home to change quick?"

Khalil glanced over at them sitting in the corner drinking their smoothies. "They'll be fine. Stop worrying, babe." Khalil lifted my chin and peered into my eyes.

"Okay, I'll try to not worry. But if your mother starts again, I won't be responsible for what comes out of my mouth." The thought whipped in so quickly of what might happen.

"Then we'll leave," Khalil said.

"Call me later and tell me all about it," Dionne said, walking out of the shop.

I got the boys settled in the car while Khalil locked up the shop. I turned the air on in the car and unlocked his side of the door.

"What did they cook for lunch?" I pressed.

"Probably some new French food recipe that my mom is

trying out." Khalil turned the volume down low on the radio station as Gladys Knight's voice came on.

I extended my hand to plant on top of his thigh as he drove. "I'm half-nervous and half-excited to see your parents again."

"Why do you say that?" Khalil interrogated and turned onto the highway with his signal light for the left lane toward the carpool lane. The sun was shining bright as he drove, and the boys continued watching their favorite cartoons on the mini iPads he had for them.

"I'm at peace with being in your life and know it doesn't matter what they think or believe. I'm not going anywhere, and I dare anyone to try to get between us." I slipped my hand out of his and reached up to caress a hand over his cheek.

He leaned into my hand and turned his head to place a kiss on my open palm. He winked as he got off the freeway and turned toward the block his parents lived on. "They seem to have come to terms with how I live my life. Never again will I allow anyone to tell me who I should love," Khalil announced and pulled into the private gated community his family lived in.

The property covered over three hundred acres of land and twenty thousand square feet. He parked the car in the driveway, and we opened the door at the same time to get out.

"You know better than that." Khalil pointed at my hand on the door.

"Sorry."

The front door opened with their butler coming down the stairs to help us with the boys.

"Hello, Miss Serena," Thomas said as he waved to Silas and Prince.

"Hi, Thomas. How are you doing?" I quizzed, reaching over and hugged him. Besides Edith and Marilyn, their housekeeper, I couldn't find one good thing about coming over here.

"I'm well, Miss Serena," Thomas spoke with a tone filled with awe and respect.

We strolled inside, Khalil and I holding the boys' hands as they looked around the spacious front entrance in awe like it was a castle.

"Your parents are inside with your brother and niece, Khalil," Thomas discussed.

All of us followed Khalil as he walked off, picking up Prince in his arms. Kayla jumped out of her grandfather's arms when she saw us and ran toward Khalil and me, hugging his legs. He dropped down to her eye level and placed Prince next to her to kiss her forehead.

"Uncle Khalil, I missed you," Kayla said, grabbing both sides of his face.

"I missed you too, princess. Are you taking care of your mom and dad?" Khalil questioned.

I glanced up at Khalil's parents, his brother, and his wife.

"Khalil, we're so happy to see you, son. How are you?" his mom said, stood and marched over to give him a kiss on the cheek.

"I'm good," Khalil replied.

Stella peered over at me and smiled. "Serena, glad to see you and the boys," Stella stated, her voice fragile and shaking.

"Glad to see you as well, Mrs. Harrison," I replied.

"Would it be okay if we go in the kitchen and catch up?" she asked.

I glanced at Khalil, and he shrugged his shoulders, letting me know that it was up to me if I wanted to talk with her or not. "Sure," I answered and followed toward the kitchen. Marilyn was cutting up some vegetables, and I waved at her.

"Marilyn, can you give me a minute with Serena alone please?" Stella checked.

"Yes, ma'am," Marilyn answered as she wiped her hands on her apron and strolled out.

"Take a seat please," Stella said as she reached for two wine glasses out of the cabinet and motioned if I wanted a glass.

I nodded.

She opened the bottle, poured a little white wine inside, and sat next to me. "I apologize," Stella said and took a sip of her wine.

I choked on the wine and slapped my chest. "Wow."

"I know I wasn't friendly toward you when I first met you at Savory, then when my son brought you to our house," Stella informed me.

"Not only you." I remembered how Mr. Harrison and even Lexi treated me.

"My husband and I feel terrible about the way we treated you in the beginning," she said.

I clasped my hands together, leaning forward. "I want you to know that I'm not leaving Khalil; my boys adore him."

"I know, and I couldn't imagine how it came across with us still being friends with Lexi," she spoke.

"That was something else."

Stella crossed her legs. "Lexi was a family friend."

"Was?" I questioned, my brow arched.

Stella looked around the kitchen and back to me. "We're no longer friends with her family. It's not worth losing our son," Stella stated.

"Are you able to accept my children?" I wondered, taking another sip of my drink.

"Of course. I love children. It might be hard to understand me, but I wasn't always like this," Stella joked.

"Really."

"I think this world gets you caught up, takes a hold of you, and wants the picture-perfect family. My husband and I tried to fit that mold," Stella said as she gulped the last of her wine and poured another glass.

"You're not alone in trying to be picture perfect. I didn't think I was good enough for Khalil either at first."

"That I can't imagine. You're a smart, beautiful girl. Any guy would be lucky to have you," Stella commented and stood.

I followed her as she headed back into the living room. "Thank you."

Stella stretched her hand. "Listen, can we start over?"

"I'd like that," I said and extended my hand for a shake.

She grasped my palm and smiled. "Ohh, and I love your cupcakes," Stella stated.

I smiled. "Thank you. I'm excited about the store opening." At the end of the day, Khalil has to deal with his parents, not me if we ever got married. I would never put myself in a situation again to be controlled.

"Khalil told us about that, and we'd love to come," Stella said.

"I'd love for you to come. I'll make sure we have some extra lemon cupcakes especially for you."

The boys were playing with Kendall as Kayla sat in her grandfather's lap and talked with Khalil. All eyes looked over at us, and I threw a thumb up that everything was fine.

"Good, so we can eat now," Samuel called out as he jumped up with Kayla in his arms. Khalil narrowed his eyes at me, and I blew a kiss at him. He swaggered over to me and kissed me on the lips.

"Ohh, Uncle Khalil, you kissed Serena," Kayla blurted out, and we all burst into laughter.

Thomas placed lunch down on the table as we each took a seat. Khalil pulled a chair out for me, and I plopped down as Silas and Prince sat across from us next to Kendall. They'd made an impression on him already, and I knew my boys probably wanted to stay with him and Kayla for the weekend.

"So, Serena, Khalil said your shop is about to open," Samuel stated, grabbing his napkin.

"It is, and we're having a grand opening party."

"She's already invited us, Samuel," Stella announced.

"If you want, I can have a few magazines and TV stations come to do some interviews," Samuel offered.

"Thank you for the offer, but Dionne is handling the party details."

"Let me know, and I'm happy to extend a hand," he said.

Khalil leaned over and kissed me on the cheek again, but I tried to push him away. "What's wrong with you?" he whispered in my ear.

I pushed him back. "Not in front of your parents."

He chuckled, and I rolled my eyes at him. Lunch came out, and they had a mixture of salads, baked chicken, peas, tacos, and steamed rice.

Khalil pointed at the food on the table. "What's this?" He scanned the table.

"We're trying to keep it simple this time, Khalil," Stella said.

"Finally," Kendall mumbled under his breath, and we all burst into laughter at his statement. Lunch lasted about two hours, and we went to the backyard afterward to watch the kids play in the treehouse built when Khalil and Kendall were younger. The day was the best I'd ever had, and I felt we'd come together as a family. I finally had the success I'd always wanted, not only personally, but professionally as well. I drove us back home, and we bathed the boys, put them to bed, and showered. In bed, we spent the rest of the night talking about our future goals and dreams we saw for ourselves as the boys got older.

21

SERENA

Early the next morning, I was baking some cupcakes fresh for the grand opening. The construction was almost done, and a few simple things still needed to be fixed before we officially opened. Hopefully, I had enough inventory and wouldn't sell out during the grand opening. Khalil stayed home with the boys and texted that he was taking them out for the day to see a movie and grab pizza with Kayla. I heard the doorbell ring, and I dropped the mixing bowl, looked toward the security camera, and saw Dionne and Nori. I removed my apron and walked out of the kitchen to the front as the construction crew continued putting shelves up on the walls and mounting the TV up on the wall.

"What brings you two here?" I crossed-examined, hugging myself.

"We wanted to check to see how things went with Khalil's parents," Nori said and stood at the front case holding the register and cupcakes.

I picked up the pieces of plastic from the boxes, tossing them in the trash. "Surprisingly, everything went well."

Dionne slid graciously into the cushioned chair in the corner. "So, his mother apologized?" Dionne asked.

"Yep, and even asked if they could come to the party."

Nori leaned against the counter. "Wow, that's big of them."

"Can we have some samples?" Dionne questioned.

"No, I have an exact amount for the party."

Dionne poked out her lip, tossing her hands in the air. "You're no fun."

I gave in and opened the case to get her and Nori a cupcake. "Here, crazy."

"I knew you loved me," Dionne joked, taking a napkin from the back counter, licking the icing from the top of the coconut cream cupcake.

I chuckled at her.

"How long do you plan to be here today?" Nori investigated.

"Not too long. I want to get home, cook dinner for the boys, and plan out the interviews for employees."

Dionne snatched up a water bottle and passed one to Nori. "Has Jaylen come around?" Dionne voiced.

"We talked the other day, and he apologized and wanted to see the boys."

"Are you going to let him?" Nori quizzed, taking a bite of the red velvet cupcake.

"I think he's finally realized I've grown from him, and I'm not depressed anymore."

"I remember when you called and moved into your parents' house right after the breakup," Dionne remarked.

"I was in a dark place but with the help of my babies, I knew I would make it somehow."

Nori slid some of the business cards in the holder, organizing some of the decor. "You sure have, and the grand opening already has a lot of people wanting to come." She approached us again.

"Khalil's father even offered to have the press come."

"I have that covered. You just enjoy the opening and the love," Dionne stated.

"To Sweet Cupcakes!" Nori yelled out, holding the half-eaten cupcake in her hand.

I laughed as Dionne did the same thing, and they lightly smashed their cupcakes together.

"Do you need anything else? I'm heading to the grocery store," Dionne commented as she tossed the last piece of cupcake in her mouth.

I studied the time on my watch and felt I could end the day and come back early if need be. "I'll head out with you to the store. I need to grab some things for dinner." I wiped the counter down, grabbed my purse from the back, and followed Dionne and Nori.

"I need to head home to check on Arvon and the boys. I'll see you at the opening, babe." Nori hugged me.

Dionne and I waved to Nori watching her leave. I jumped in my car and followed Dionne to the grocery store.

...

Ten minutes later, we pulled into the parking lot of Publix, and I parked my car next to Dionne. As we entered the store, we talked about all the last-minute items we'd need for the party.

"Do you need any meats?" I sounded out, pushing the cart in that section.

Dionne grabbed a small basket. "I need to get a few pieces of fish," she said.

"How are things with the boyfriend?" I watched her check the prices.

Dionne glanced over the frozen food area. "Really good. He's off today."

"Khalil said he's going to have another poker night with the guys if your man wants to attend," I declared, looking over the batches of fresh vegetables.

I heard a loud, familiar laugh and turned to my right, only to see Lexi looking like she was coming from a fashion show, standing next to a guy in a suit. She leaned up against him, patting his chest.

"What do you think of this price?" Dionne pressed, pushing the chicken and fish in front of my face.

"Should I say something?" I muttered as I motioned toward Lexi and her date.

"What are you—" Dionne started to look.

I waved her off. "Don't stare."

"I'm not worried about that girl. You shouldn't either. Khalil wants you and loves the boys," Dionne said.

"You're right."

Dionne snapped her finger, grabbing a few vegetables. "I know I'm right. Ignore her and pray for the guy leaning against her that he doesn't end up broke trying to date her," Dionne joked.

I chuckled, pointed to the fish that she should buy, and we continued on down the row of vegetables. I guess we weren't a factor to her anymore because Lexi completely ignored us as we passed by her. Fifteen minutes later, I paid at the register and drove back home feeling like a huge weight had lifted off my shoulders. I pulled into the garage and grabbed the two bags of groceries. I heard loud laughter as I stepped into the kitchen through the garage and saw Edith at the sink, washing dishes.

"Hey, Serena," Edith stated, grabbing one of the bags out of my hands.

"Hi. I'm going to cook dinner tonight, so you can relax and have the night off."

"Are you sure?" Edith questioned.

"You work hard all the time, and the boys are probably stuffed from the pizza. I'll make something light for dinner."

"Okay. I'd love to get an early nap in for the day. Boys wore me out yesterday." Edith laughed, and I joined in, knowing how they would keep her going with questions and running around.

"Are you able to come to the party?" I questioned.

"I'd love to come," Edith said.

"Perfect! Well, have a good night and don't worry about breakfast tomorrow either."

"Have I mentioned that you're the best thing that has ever happened to Khalil?" Edith remarked and hugged me tight as I chuckled.

"That goes both ways."

Khalil walked into the kitchen, wrapped his arms around me, and kissed the side of my cheek. "How was your day?" Khalil pressed.

"It was busy, trying to finish setting things up. I did leave early to grab groceries for dinner."

Khalil grabbed bags from my hands. "We could have ordered out. The boys will probably be ready for bed in a minute." He laid them on the table.

"What did you guys do today?"

He removed his hands from around me, went to the fridge, and grabbed a bottle of water. "I took them to the park, then a movie, and out for pizza." Khalil sipped the water.

"How tired are you?" I teased, rubbing his shoulders.

"Exhausted, I won't lie. Having three kids wanting to play different video games at the same time in the pizza joint was insane," Khalil explained.

"Poor baby. You want me to give you a massage?"

He placed the glass in the sink, helping me. "I'm good. Do you need help with anything?" He let out a long exhalation of relief.

"No, dinner will be ready soon. I planned to make chili tonight."

Khalil rubbed his stomach and grinned, loving my homemade chili. "I'll let you get to it and watch the boys," Khalil said.

"Thanks, baby," I replied and kissed him on the lips.

An hour later, we finished dinner, sat in the theater room, and watched one of the scary movies he loved as I curled up next to him.

"I saw Lexi today."

He nodded, never taking his eyes off the movie. "Did she say anything to you?"

"No. I was with Dionne, and we walked past her. She was with some guy. Looked like they were on a date."

Khalil slid an arm around me. "Good for her." His steady gaze bore into me.

"She was dressed like she came off the runway," I commented, running my hand over the back of his head.

"I wouldn't put anything past her. Would you want to open a second shop?" Khalil changed the subject.

"I don't know. I have to hire enough staff, and it depends on the sales."

"My company is investing in businesses. I see potential in your brand, baby," Khalil advised.

"Thank you, baby, but let me see how things go first. I

will let you know if I need your help," I said as we continued talking about things happening at his office until the movie had us both drifting off on the couch.

22

KHALIL

Two weeks later.

I was preparing to leave work to pick up the boys and then meet Serena at her shop to head to dinner. My parents finally were on the same page with what I chose for my life, especially wanting Serena to be my wife one day. I picked up the ring from the safe in my office, and I planned to propose at the party in front of our family and friends. I turned my computer off and grabbed my briefcase and jacket to leave for the day. It was almost two-thirty, and they should be ready to go.

"Leaving for the day, sir?" Antoine asked.

I verified my watch again.

"Yeah, hold all my calls until tomorrow."

"Sounds good," Antoine said.

"Thanks," I replied and hit the button for the elevator. I was thinking of promoting Antoine to handle his own accounts to help cut down my workload so I could spend more time with the kids and Serena. The doors opened, and I motioned to security that I was leaving for the day. Lexi hadn't come by ever since Serena confronted her about trying to break us up. It was laughable to me now how far things had progressed for me and Serena, all from a broken-down car on the freeway. I was now about to become someone's husband and the stepfather to two boys. I got in my car and backed out of the employee space. I stopped at the light as my Bluetooth went off, flashing Serena's name.

"Hey," I said, pulling off as the light turned green.

"How's your day going?" Serena inquired.

"I'm leaving the office now to pick up the boys," I answered.

"Thank you again for doing this for me," Serena spoke.

"You don't have to thank me. I'm a part of their lives because I know you come as a package deal," I replied.

"Do you think this party is too much?" Serena wondered. I turned down Main Street, about a block from the school, and stopped as the carpool lane started.

"I think it's a good idea, and Dionne is handling all the details. You just need to show up."

"I know, but I'm so nervous. What if my sales are crap right out of the gate?" Serena whined.

"You can't think like that. As long as you put your all into the business, it'll be a success," I answered, then pulled up. All the teachers and Gladys knew me as Kayla's uncle, so it wasn't that big of a surprise when I picked them up the first time a few weeks ago. Talking with Nori, Gladys waved as she walked the boys over to my car.

"The boys are about to get in the car, babe. I'll call you back," I said.

"Okay," Serena replied. "Give them both a kiss for me."

"I will and stop stressing. If it fails, which I doubt because everyone raves about your cupcakes, it fails. Hell, even my mom wanted you to make them for my wedding."

"That's not funny, Khalil," Serena grunted.

The back passenger door opened. Silas and Prince excitedly said hello and fist bumped me.

"How's she holding up?" Nori questioned.

"I'm not," Serena blurted out through the Bluetooth.

I chuckled.

"Stop worrying, Serena. You're the best, and I can't wait for the grand opening," Nori encouraged.

"I keep telling her that, and she doesn't believe me."

"Hi, Mommy!" Prince and Silas spoke at the same time.

"Hi, boys. Be good for Khalil, and I will see you soon," Serena said before we ended the call.

"How were they today?" I asked Nori.

"They were good as usual. Silas, remember to bring your permission slip for the field trip." Nori handed me the form for Serena to sign so they could go to the aquarium.

"Thanks, Nori. Tell Arvon we'll catch up tonight," I told her, driving away, heading home.

"Khalil, are you and Mommy getting married?" Prince questioned.

"That's something you have to ask your mom, buddy. Hopefully, I get the chance to one day call her my wife," I answered.

Fighting my smile, we made it home, and I told them to go upstairs and change. I had lunch already prepared to hold them over until the party tonight. I went upstairs into my bedroom to shower and change when I heard the water running already. I walked into the bathroom and saw Serena standing naked under the water with a smile on her face.

"How did you get here so fast?" I questioned, removing my jacket and tie then kicking off my shoes.

"Dionne has everything under control at the shop, so I

wanted to come back and get refreshed," Serena explained, holding her hand out for me.

"The boys are awake."

"They'll be fine for a few minutes. I need some alone time with you." Serena grabbed the lavender bar and a towel.

"You know how loud you can get, baby."

"Shut up and get in here." Serena chuckled.

I stepped in, pulling her into my arms. I moved her back against the wall under the hot stream of water. "I like hearing you call out my name."

"I love calling out your name too," Serena teased and stood on her tippy-toes to kiss me on the lips.

I gripped her ass and lifted her up as I lined up with her entrance. I held her at only the tip as she leaned down and nudged her face in my neck. I pushed in further right as banging on our bathroom door interrupted us. "Fuck!" I groaned, letting her down on her feet.

"Sorry, we can finish after the party," Serena taunted as she gripped my dick.

"That's not funny," I grumbled, then rolled my eyes as she laughed while the boys continued knocking.

"I'm coming!" Serena shouted, walking around me to grab the towel and talk to the boys. I stood underneath the water, closed my eyes, and handled it as I thought of Serena bent over my desk as my secretary.

...

By the time we got back, the music blasted inside Sweet Cupcakes as her parents talked with the boys near the chocolate bar. Dionne managed certain sections around the shop from a photo booth to candy cane lane. Savory catered a bar for the adults and finger snacks, and even though Wasim couldn't make it, she did have a few coworkers like Eboan, Maahir, and Uliana roaming around. Nori and Arvon walked inside with Graham and Jett.

"The place looks great." Nori glanced around the room. I shook hands with Arvon and slapped hands with Graham and Jett. I pointed to the kids near the chocolate stand, and they asked Arvon if they could go over to grab some cookies and cupcakes.

"I know, and she's still nervous."

"Once the doors open, she'll be fine," Arvon spoke.

"How are you guys doing?" I asked.

"Good, busy with work and life. The kids keep us busy," Nori stated.

"That'll be you soon, once you propose," Arvon reminded me, and I checked for the ring inside my pocket.

"I wanted to do it when we had dinner, but with all of her friends and family here, I think this is the best time," I told them.

"She deserves happiness," Nori remarked.

"Is Jaylen giving you problems anymore?" Arvon questioned.

"Not anymore. Thanks for that information on the lawyer. I know you went through the same issues with your ex," I stated, and I noticed the grimace across his face at the mention of Beth.

"Don't remind me," Arvon remarked, and Nori rubbed a hand up his back.

"Khalil, are you ready?" Dionne came over and said to me.

"Yeah, once she gives a speech and opens the doors."

Dionne nodded as she pulled the mic up to speak. "Ladies and gentlemen, can I have your attention?" Dionne asked. The DJ stopped the music, and Serena turned from her mother to look up at Dionne. I watched her in her element as her dreams came true from all of her hard work.

"Serena, come up here please," Dionne said.

"Dionne, we don't have all day for long speeches," Serena kidded, and the room erupted in laughter.

"I won't be long." Dionne grabbed the other mic for Serena to talk.

"So, I know you've worked hard for this, and I'm super proud of you, my friend. I just wanted you to know that this is the beginning of many more wonderful things to happen for you and the boys. Sweet Cupcakes is your baby, and I remember the first time I told you that you couldn't go wrong with selling them."

"I remember; you basically said why are you not making this into a business?" Serena mimicked Dionne.

"And now look at you, about to open your own business, and you've found love along the way," Dionne mentioned, and that was my cue to step up and grab the mic from her.

"Thanks, Dionne," I said as Serena looked surprised at me moving up on the stage.

"What are you doing, Khalil?" Serena whispered in my ear.

"Serena, we met in the oddest of ways, and I tell you all the time, I normally don't stop when a car is broken down," I told her.

"We did... I didn't like you at first," Serena joked, and the room burst into laughter.

"You were a challenge, and I'm glad you gave me a chance to get to know you and the boys."

"They love you more than me," Serena pouted.

Silas yelled, "Love you, Mommy."

"Thank you, Silas," Serena said.

I dropped down to one knee, and she gasped in shock. I lifted her left hand up. "Will you marry me and make me the luckiest guy in the world?" I pulled the ring out of my pocket.

She teared up and nodded her head in answer.

"Is that a yes?" I asked.

"Yes! I'll marry you," Serena shouted.

I slid the ring on her finger as our family and friends cheered and screamed. I stood and devoured her lips, wrapping my arms around her waist.

"All right, we have kids here. Save all that for later," Dionne commented.

We backed away from each other.

"When did you do this?" Serena questioned, looking at the ring.

"I've wanted to marry you since the second we had our first official date, but I knew from the ice cream shop, you'd be mine. Was just a matter of time until you came around," I said as I pecked her lips again.

She rubbed the red lipstick off, and the boys ran over to the stage. I lifted Prince up, as she had Silas in her arms.

"Can I call you Daddy now?" Prince asked, and the room got quiet.

"You can call me whatever you like. I'm never leaving you," I spoke and kissed his cheek.

"Okay, we need to open those doors. It's time. Serena, are you ready?" Dionne announced, standing next to the front door.

"Yep, I'm ready to start now. I just wanted to say thank you all for believing in me," Serena explained.

"We love you, Serena!" her mom yelled.

"You rock, Mommy!" Silas shouted.

Serena laughed at his outburst.

Dionne opened the doors, and the crowd walked inside as the DJ started the music back up, and the kids ran to the section by the chocolate fountain. I put Prince back down on the floor and nudged Serena to put Silas down so he could play. I pulled Serena to a side corner near her office as everyone enjoyed watching the boys dance.

"You really want to marry me?" Serena asked as she pressed her hand against my chest.

I moved her against the wall, putting my hands on both sides of her, and lowered my head to kiss her lips.

"I want you, Silas, and Prince in my life forever," I stated.

"You got us," Serena said, as she lifted her arms around my neck and pulled me into another make out session. A few minutes later, we walked back to the party and talked with customers. Serena showed off her ring to Dionne and Nori. I stood off to the side and watched the wide smile on her face as we came full circle.

"You look just like I did with Nori," Arvon said.

"What is that?" I grabbed a bottle of water from the bar.

"The look of a man in love who will do anything for his woman," Arvon remarked.

"Until Serena, I didn't know what love was," I spoke.

Arvon smirked at me as both our women walked toward us. I grasped Serena's waist and kissed behind her ear.

EPILOGUE: SERENA

Two years later

It was bright out with the sun shining, and the kids laughing and playing in the backyard. The barbecue grill was going while our friends and family came together and played in the pool. I was content in my life after so many years of struggling, trying to figure out life as a single mom of two boys. Wondering how I would keep them in a place of innocence and not make it harder by having people running in and out of their lives. Even repairing my relationship with my parents was a long road, but they'd made the biggest turnaround, loving the kids and showing up whenever we needed them. Now, here I was, getting ready to open a second bakery next month, married, and about to have another child. I was worried at first when I found out I was pregnant because having another set of twins would have driven me crazy. I smiled and looked at KJ running behind his big brothers. Seven months ago, he started walking, and we couldn't keep up with him. He tried his best to hide so he didn't get caught destroying our house. I felt strong hands wrap around my waist and rub a palm across my stomach.

"How are you feeling?" Khalil pressed.

I leaned my head against his shoulder. "I'm good, ready to eat and be alone with you."

"If you want, I can kick everybody out and take you upstairs for a hot bath and rub your feet," Khalil suggested as he arched his left brow at me. That would only lead to us being in bed, having sex. As soon as we got engaged, I found out I was pregnant with Khalil, Jr. aka little KJ. Khalil was over the moon with being a dad and practically wouldn't let me do anything, from changing diapers to feedings. He had KJ spoiled rotten, and both our parents wanted to keep him overnight, only he didn't approve until he started walking. Here I was again, pregnant with our second baby and my fourth altogether. One thing I could say about him was that he made sure Silas and Prince never felt like they weren't as much of a priority as KJ. Anything one child had, he made sure all the kids were given the same.

"Serena, do you mind if I take the boys for the weekend?" Jaylen walked over and asked. Silas and Prince ran around the bouncy house, laughing as KJ chased them down.

"No, that's fine. They'd love to spend the weekend with their brothers and sisters," I stated.

"That gives us a break, if we can send KJ with my parents," Khalil joked.

I laughed.

Jaylen and I came to an agreement after going to counseling and mediation. Khalil was hesitant at first, but over time, they'd gotten along better, not to say they were friends. I knew Silas and Prince constantly talked about Khalil with

Jaylen, so he knew he was here to stay, and they loved him as much as they loved their biological dad.

"I can't believe how fast they've grown up," Jaylen remarked.

"Two eight-year-old boys. Next, they'll be sixteen and ready to drive." I watched them all play.

Khalil laid a hand on my lower back. "I already know what car they want."

"Did Silas tell you he has a girlfriend?" Jaylen told me.

"My baby does not have a girlfriend." I walked toward him and found out what little girl was getting into his head. Khalil and Jaylen laughed at me as Khalil pulled me back into his arms.

"Baby, you can't stop every girl who comes across him. You just have to teach him how to be a gentleman and let him be a kid," Khalil explained.

"Fine, but the second I find out her name, I'm telling her parents."

"Stop worrying," Khalil said.

"Thanks again, Serena. I know things aren't ideal, but I'm grateful that you let me back into their lives," Jaylen said and hugged me with one arm, since Khalil wasn't letting me go.

I chortled as Jaylen walked off, and Khalil kept his eyes narrowed on me.

"What?" Khalil questioned.

"You are a mess. I'm pregnant with swollen feet, and you're jealous over a hug?"

"So, you're mine, and I want everyone to know that. Besides, you look beautiful to me," Khalil said.

"Thanks, baby."

"Serena Harrison... I'm thankful for you, baby." Khalil kissed my forehead and squeezed me around the waist as the kids ran over to my dad on the grill to get their hamburgers. Jaylen's wife helped them grab a drink and chips and sat them down next to their siblings on the bench as Jaylen talked with Arvon and Nori. My life wasn't perfect, but it was complete, and I wouldn't change anything for the world.

I hope you enjoyed **Serena** and **Khalil's story.** If you want to see more of these characters, then check out bonus scenes here: https://chiquitadennie.squarespace.com/bonus-scenes, and start another series from the beginning with Kash and Arianna.

Ethan and Maya has a story to tell in **Bossy Billionaire** here: https://bit.ly/3uB5oBC

Follow the TN Seal Security series with the standalone, opposites-attract, fake-dating, military romance **Nicco** here: https://bit.ly/47ZZN6p

Are you a fan of sports romance? Then download the one-night stand, billionaire romance **Refuel** here: https://bit.ly/3RqFx8l

Also, follow it up with the workplace, sports romance **Pressure** here: https://bit.ly/3RqagT1

If you love romantic comedy, fake relationships, and enemies-to-lovers, then find it in **Something Gained** here: https://bit.ly/3OwGbiP.

My stories of friends finding love started with the Heart of Stone series, which includes a host of characters and families. It starts with **Broken** (Emery and Jackson, Book 1), a sports, one-night-stand, workplace romance found here: https://bit.ly/3hxVavF

Then you can continue with a fun side-story about Emery

and Jackson with their **Valentine's Day Short** here: https://bit.ly/42ttg7o

Emery's best friend Jordan's story continues in **Rebirth** (Book 2), a single-dad, widow, billionaire romance: https://bit.ly/3YiQtGS

Hop on and download **Reveal** with Angela and Brent here: https://bit.ly/3OupYur

If you love bonus content, then click here for bonus scenes: https://chiquitadennie.squarespace.com/bonus-scenes

Please also check out a second-chance, workplace romance with a host of characters intertwined in **Renew** (Book 4) here: https://bit.ly/3wOrgHi

Follow Desiree and Gabriel in **Temptation,** a standalone, contemporary, sports, curvy girl romance here: https://bit.ly/42r8ODQ

Check out the dark mafia romance that started my journey with Antonio and Sabrina in **Ruthless** (Book 1) here: https://bit.ly/3iS64XT

Antonio and Sabrina's relationship continues in **Savage** (Book 2), as they get to know each other and their families here: https://bit.ly/3w77CJT

Antonio and Sabrina have more work to do in **Beast** (Book 3) here: https://bit.ly/3Untivm

Did you know that **Janice and Carlo** have a book? Well, grab this dark mafia romance with emotional scars and betrayal here: https://bit.ly/42yJBaH

Any fans of forbidden political romance? Check out the steamy romance **Mutual Agreement** here: https://bit.ly/3OyAzod

Do you love workplace romantic suspense? Then check out **Aydin** here: https://bit.ly/496jKcv

Also, check out the interconnected standalone, hate-to-love, damsel-in-distress, actress-and-bodyguard romance **Nasir** here: https://bit.ly/3uovwQr

Have you checked out **She's All I Need,** a sports, opposites-attract romance? Click here: https://books2read.com/u/49lkeW

How about a dark romance that has everything, from steamy romance to opposites-attract, suspense, thriller, celebrities, and more? Read **Stolen** (Book 1) here: https://books2read.com/u/mvZlgV

Don't miss Joaquin and Sofia's follow-up story in **Saved** (Book 2) here: https://books2read.com/u/4DWwLd

The conclusion for Joaquin and Sofia comes full circle in **Betrayed** (Book 3) here: https://books2read.com/u/4A5LGp

Catch up with your favorite characters in the holiday short romance (includes spoilers) **Holiday Collection** here: https://books2read.com/u/bzd59G

For small-town, single-mom stories, check out **Until Seren**a here: https://books2read.com/u/mej8vr

Do you love fun billionaire romances? If so, then check out **Cocky Catcher**, a sports, enemies-to-lovers romance, here: https://bit.ly/3R57VeT

Are you a reader of sports workplace romance? Then grab **Scoring with Sadie**, a workplace, enemies-to-lovers romance, here: https://bit.ly/3nkWhBp

All curvy girl, plus-size romance lovers should get into **I Deserve His Love,** a standalone, second-chance romance here: https://books2read.com/u/mVrGwP

Finally, fantasy romance readers should look no further than **Red Light District**, a curvy girl, fling romance: https://books2read.com/u/m2RQ6G

A NOTE TO READERS

Hello!

If you enjoyed this story please share on social media and spread the word in a review and ratings. The support helps to showcase my work into bigger audiences. If you come across any errors please notify me by email info@ chiqutiadennie.com

CATALOG OF RELEASES

Series

Struck in Love

The Early Years-A Prequel Short Story

Ruthless: Antonio and Sabrina Book 1

Savage: Antonio and Sabrina Book 2

Beast: Antonio and Sabrina Book 3

Captivated By His Love: Janice and Carlo

Brutal: Antonio and Sabrina Booke 4

Redemption: Antonio and Sabrina Book 5

Heart of Stone

Broken, Book 1 (Emery & Jackson)

A Valentine's Day Short Book 1.5 Emery & Jackson

Rebirth, Book 2 (Jordan and Damon)

Reveal, Book 3 (Angela and Brent)

Bottoms Up Book 3.5 Jessica and Joseph Short

Renew, Book 4 (Jessica and Joseph)

Cocky Billionaire Boys

Cocky Catcher (Cocky Billionaire Boys Book 1)

 Catalog of Releases

Bossy Billionaire (Cocky Billionaire Boys Book 2)

The Fuertes Cartel

Stolen (The Fuertes Cartel Book 1)
Saved (The Fuertes Cartel Book 2)
Betrayed (The Fuertes Cartel Book 3)

Carrington Cartel

Torn: The Carrington Cartel Book 1
Claim: The Carrington Cartel Book 2

Something

Something Gained: A Romantic Comedy Book 1
Something Earned: A Romantic Comedy Book 2

Pierce Motors

Refuel:(Pierce Motors Book 1)
Pressure:(Pierce Motors Book 2)
Ride: (Pierce Motors Book 3)

Summer Break

Summer Nights (Summer Break Book 1)

TN Seal Security

Aydin: Book 1
Nasir: Book 2
Nicco: Book 3

TN Seal Security Nashville Division

Protecting Bria: Book 1
Protecting Chanel: Book 2
Protecting Yanira: Book 3

Standalones

Until Serena (HEA World Novel)
Temptation
She's All I Need
I Deserve His Love
Mutual Agreement
Scoring with Sadie
Exposed (A Bodyguard Novel)
Love Shorts: A Collection of Short Stories
Red Light District (A Fantasy Romance Short)

ABOUT THE AUTHOR

Chiquita Dennie is an author of contemporary, romantic suspense, erotic, and women's fiction.

Chiquita lives in Los Angeles, CA. Before she started writing contemporary romance, she worked in the entertainment industry on notable TV shows such as the Dr Phil show, Tyra Banks Show, American Idol, and Deal or No Deal. But her favorite job is the one she's now doing, full-time writing romance.

A best-selling author and award-winning filmmaker, her first short film "Invisible" was released in Summer 2017 and screened in multiple festivals and won for Best Short Film. She also hosts a podcast that showcases the latest in beauty, business and community called "Moscato and Tea." Her debut release of *Antonio and Sabrina Struck in Love* has opened a new avenue of writing that she loves.

If you want to know when the next book will come out, please visit my website at http://www.chiquitadennie.com, where you can sign up to receive an email for my next release.

ACKNOWLEDGE

I want to say thank you to everyone who helped me on the project from the cover designer, to editor, beta readers, and proofreaders. I appreciate your continued support.

WHAT'S NEXT?!

Want to know what happens next?

Follow me on social media to catch the next release.

Reviews are the lifeblood of the publishing world. They're read, appreciated, and needed. Please consider taking the time to leave a few words on Goodreads, or BookBub.

Sign up for updates and sneak peaks at the site below.

www.bookbub.com/chiquitadennie

www.304publishing.com

www.chiquitadennie.com

www.goodreads.com/author/chiquitadennie

www.Twitter.com/304_publishing

www.Instagram.com/304publishing

www.Facebook.com/authorchiquitadennie

www.304publishing.tumblr.com

Thank you so much for reading and if you enjoyed the crazy ride and decide to leave a review, we appreciate the support.

www.ingramcontent.com/pod-product-compliance
Lightning Source LLC
Chambersburg PA
CBHW070921190726
48292CB00004B/1059